What can you expect in Harlequin Presents?

Passionate relationships

Revenge and redemption

Emotional intensity

Seduction

Escapist, glamorous settings from around the world

New stories every month

The most handsome and successful heroes

Scores of internationally bestselling writers

Find all this in our November books—on sale now!

Men who can't be tamed...or so they think!

If you love strong, commanding men,
you'll love this miniseries.

Meet the guy who breaks the rules to get
exactly what he wants, because he is...

HARD-EDGED & HANDSOME
He's the man who's impossible to resist...

RICH & RAKISH
He's got everything—and needs nobody...
Until he meets one woman...

He's RUTHLESS!
In his pursuit of passion; in his world
the winner takes all!

Brought to you by your favorite
Harlequin Presents® authors!

Coming next month:

Pleasured in the Billionaire's Bed
by Miranda Lee
#2588

Trish Morey

A VIRGIN FOR
THE TAKING

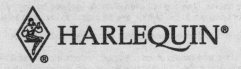

TORONTO • NEW YORK • LONDON
AMSTERDAM • PARIS • SYDNEY • HAMBURG
STOCKHOLM • ATHENS • TOKYO • MILAN • MADRID
PRAGUE • WARSAW • BUDAPEST • AUCKLAND

ISBN-13: 978-0-373-12585-2
ISBN-10:   0-373-12585-2

A VIRGIN FOR THE TAKING

First North American Publication 2006.

www.eHarlequin.com

Printed in U.S.A.

All about the author…
Trish Morey

TRISH MOREY wrote her first book at age eleven for a children's book-week competition. Entitled *Island Dreamer,* it proved to be her first rejection. Shattered and broken, she turned to a life where she could combine her love of fiction with her need for creativity—and became a chartered accountant. Life wasn't all dull though, as she embarked on a skydiving course, completing three jumps before deciding that she'd given her fear of heights a run for its money.

Meanwhile, she fell in love and married a handsome guy who cut computer code. After the birth of their second daughter, Trish spied an article saying that Harlequin was actively seeking new authors. It was one of those eureka moments—Trish was going to be one of those authors!

Eleven years after reading that fateful article, the magical phone call came and Trish finally realized her dream. According to Trish, writing and selling a book is a major life achievement that ranks right up there with jumping out of an airplane and motherhood. All three take commitment, determination and sheer guts, but the effort is so very, very worthwhile.

Trish now lives with her husband and four young daughters in a special part of south Australia, surrounded by orchards and bushland and visited by the occasional koala and kangaroo.

You can visit Trish at her Web site at www.trishmorey.com or e-mail her at trish@trishmorey.com.

You really can't travel to a place like Broome, Western Australia, without burning to set a book there. Set between the stunning Kimberley and the turquoise Indian Ocean, the town imparts a real sense of drama, romance and passion. It's a fascinating town, with a fascinating history, marked by isolation, incredible hardships, colorful characters and the quest for riches—first by the collection of pearl shell for mother-of-pearl, but more recently for the cultivation of the magnificent South Sea pearls themselves, truly the most beautiful pearls in the world.

This book is dedicated to the town of Broome and to its people, a special breed for a very special place.

And very special thanks to the moon, for doing its thing that cloud-free night by rising spectacularly over the tidal flats of Roebuck Bay and making that wonderfully special phenomenon, the Stairway to the Moon.

Simply the most romantic place on earth.

Simply magic!

CHAPTER ONE

ZANE BASTIANI stepped on to the tarmac of Broome International Airport and felt the late wet-season humidity close around him like a vice. He glanced skyward in irritation, to where the source of the melting heat shone so unforgivingly above.

He'd forgotten about the heat. Other things had slipped his mind, too—like the sharp blue of the sky, the clear salt-tinged air and the sheer quality of the light. Nine years of dreary London weather and grey concrete architecture had disarmed him completely. He felt like a foreigner in his home town.

Nine years.

Hard to believe it was so long since he'd left with just his name and the conviction to make it big time on his own. Not that he'd wasted a minute of it. Now, with a terrace house in Chelsea, a chalet in Klosters and the chairmanship of the most aggressive merchant bank in London, he was well on his way.

And for every one of those nine years he'd been waiting for his father to call and admit that he'd been wrong, but when the call had finally come it hadn't been from his father at all.

'Not critical,' the doctor had assured him, 'but Laurence asked to see you.'

He'd asked to see Zane.

It might have taken a heart attack, but after all the bitterness between them, any request had to be worth something.

So Zane had taken the first flight out of London to anywhere that might offer the fastest connection with this remote north-west Australian location. His platinum credit card had taken care of the details.

He shrugged the kinks out of his shoulders as he headed for the terminal, steeling himself for meeting his father once again. When Zane had been just a kid growing up, Laurence Bastiani had always seemed larger than life, always the big man with the big voice and the big ideas who'd never succumbed to as much as the common cold. It made sense that it would take something like a heart attack to stop him in his tracks. Even so, it was impossible to picture him now, lying ill in hospital. His father would hate it. He'd probably have checked himself out of there already.

Inside the arrivals' terminal, ceiling fans spun languidly overhead, stirring up barely more than a breeze as travel-weary passengers began to crowd around the luggage carousel.

His one hastily packed leather bag, its red *Priority* tag swinging, came through first. He reached down, hauling it from the carousel, then headed towards the exit, making for the line of waiting taxis, increasingly aware the fine cotton of his shirt was already heavy with perspiration.

How long would it take to re-acclimatise to Broome's tropical temperatures, given he'd been away so many years? Not that it really mattered, he thought dismissively as he curled himself into a taxi and snapped out a brisk command to the driver. He'd be back in London long before there was any chance of that happening.

CHAPTER TWO

THE CRASH TEAM had departed, the tubes and needles removed, the equipment turned off. Strange—she'd grown to hate that incessant beeping of the monitor over the last couple of days with its constant reminder of Laurence's increasingly frail condition. But right now Ruby Clemenger would give anything to have that noise back—anything to break the deathly quiet of the room—anything at all if it meant that Laurence was still really here.

But Laurence was gone.

Her eyes felt scratchy and swollen, but there were no tears, not yet, because it was just so hard to accept. And so unfair. Fifty-five was way too young to die, especially when you had the vision and energy of Laurence Bastiani, the now late head of the largest cultured South Sea pearl operation in the world.

Even now he looked like he was sleeping, his hand still warm in hers. But there was no tell-tale rise and fall of his chest under the sheet, no flicker of eyelashes as if he was merely dreaming, no answering squeeze of his fingers.

She let her head fall forward on her chest, her eyelids jammed together as she tried to see past the yawning pit of despair inside her. But logic had deserted her tonight just as swiftly as Laurence's unexpected departure. And now all she could think about were his final words to her, half whispered, half choked, his fingers pressing urgently into her flesh as the attack that had finally taken his life overcame him.

'Look after him,' he'd managed to whisper. 'Look after Zane. And tell him—I'm sorry…'

And then the monitor's note had changed into one continual bleep and her thoughts had turned to panic. A heartbeat later the doors to the room had crashed open to a flurry of blue cotton and trolleyed machinery and in one swift blur she'd been expertly manoeuvred outside.

By the time they'd let her back in it was over and she'd never had a chance to ask him what he'd meant and why the son who hadn't bothered to contact his father the best part of a decade should need looking after or why Laurence felt he was the one who should apologise for his son's neglect. And she'd never had a chance to demand to know why the hell Laurence would expect her to be the one to do it.

But she had no time to squander on the prodigal son. After the way he'd neglected his father, Zane was so low on her radar he didn't register. Right now she'd lost her mentor, a father figure and an inspiration. Most of all, she'd lost a dear friend.

'Oh, Laurence,' she whispered, her voice cracking under the strain. 'I'll miss you so much.'

The door swung open behind her. She sniffed and took a calming breath. The staff would be wanting her to leave so they could complete the formalities. She lifted her head to acknowledge their presence.

'I'm almost ready,' she said, only half turning towards the door. 'Just a moment longer, if that's okay.'

There was no immediate response, no drawing back and closing of doors, and a strange feeling of unease crawled its way up her spine. Her back straightened in reaction, her arms prickling into goosebumps as the room chilled to ice-cold.

'I'd prefer to visit with my father alone.'

Her head snapped around to where the stranger with the ice-cold tone filled the doorway. And yet, for the briefest second, her heart skipped with recognition—until harsh reality resurfaced, snuffing out her momentary joy.

Oh, they might have been Laurence's eyes she'd been staring at, with their same dark caramel richness, the same shape and heavy-hooded, almost seductive lids. But whereas the older man's eyes had been filled with a mixture of affection and respect, their corners crinkled with laughter over a shared joke or with natural delight at discovering the perfect pearl, the eyes turned upon her now were cold and imperious.

Zane, she realised, her first-impression sensors screaming a red-light warning. *So what that he was Laurence's son?— clearly that didn't make him her friend.*

His body language made that more than plain. His unyielding stance was imbued with antagonism, from his unshaven jaw and short finger-combed dark hair to his designer black jeans and hand-crafted leather boots, planted on the tiled floor like they owned it. Even the contrasting white shirt failed to soften the impression, instead only emphasising his olive skin and dark features. He wore power like a birthright.

She forced her aching back ramrod straight in her chair as his icy gaze swept over her, noticing when it finally came to a halt where her fingers rested, still curled around his father's hand. Disapproval came off him in waves, but she pointedly maintained her hold. She had a right to be here even if he didn't like it. And he obviously didn't. Too bad.

And yet, whatever his faults, part of her recognized that he had to be hurting, too. Despite the two not speaking for years, his father's death must still have come as a huge shock. Even just one day ago Laurence had been expected to make a complete recovery, so when Zane had boarded that plane from London, the prospect of his father's death would have been a remote and unlikely possibility. He would have to be made of granite not to be affected by what he'd discovered once he'd arrived. Nobody could be that hard. Nobody could that insensitive.

'You must be Zane,' she said, trying to steer some kind of course through the jagged ice floes cluttering the atmosphere between them. 'I'm Ruby Clemenger. I worked with your father.'

'I know who you are,' he snapped.

She blinked and took a steadying breath, instantly rethinking her earlier assumption. Maybe he was that hard and insensitive, after all.

'I am sorry about your father,' she persisted, trying again, if only for Laurence's sake, because even if she didn't give a rat's about Zane, she'd wanted so much for Laurence to have his last wish met. She shook her head. 'He wanted so much to see you. But you're too late.'

His eyes narrowed in on hers, intensifying their laser-like quality.

'Too late?' he repeated. 'Oh, yeah, it sure looks that way from where I'm standing.'

She shivered in the frosty atmosphere. Why did she get the distinct impression he was talking about more than his father's untimely death?

Zane battled to hold his mounting irritation in check. *Trust her to be here.* He hadn't seen a single photograph of his father over the last few years that hadn't also featured this woman clinging to his arm. Ruby Clemenger—his father's constant companion, his father's right-hand woman. His father had always been a leg man, and, judging by the long sweep of golden limbs tucked beneath her on the armchair, nothing much had changed.

But right now all he wanted was for her to use those legs to get out of here. This was his father, his grief, *his anger*. He'd travelled the best part of twenty-four hours, only to be cheated out of seeing his father by one. He didn't want to share this time with anyone, let alone with the likes of her.

At last it seemed she was taking the hint. The spark of fight that had flared in her azure eyes had dimmed as she unwound herself out of the chair, her movements slow and deliberate, like she'd been sitting too long. But still she didn't move away from the bed, her filmy skirt floating just above knee length.

Even in their jet-lagged state his eyes couldn't help but notice—he'd been right about the legs. But now she was standing, it was clear her attributes didn't stop there—they extended much further north, an alluring mix of feminine curves and sun-kissed skin, of blue eyes framed by dark lashes and lips generous enough to be begging to be kissed—just the way he liked them.

Just the way his father liked them.

Bitterness congealed like a lead weight inside him. She had to be at least three decades younger than Laurence's fifty-five years; with a body and a face like hers, his father hadn't stood a chance—she was a heart attack waiting to happen!

As he watched, she lifted the hand she'd been holding and pressed it to her lips before gently replacing it at Laurence's side. Then she leaned over and smoothed a thumb over his brow. He watched her dip her head, the loose tendrils of her whisky-coloured hair falling free of the clasp at the back of her head as she kissed his father on the cheek one final time.

'Goodbye, Laurence,' he heard her whisper. 'I'll always love you.'

The words struck him like a blow deep in a place already overflowing with rancour and tainted by a cynicism borne from working on some of the ugliest corporate take-overs in Europe.

Her performance was no doubt all for his benefit. He knew what people were capable of when there were fortunes at stake.

Ruby Clemenger was merely an employee of the Bastiani Pearl Corporation, although clearly her 'duties' extended way beyond her jewellery design. Of course, she would know the Corporation was worth hundreds of millions of dollars. Would she hope to establish there was more to the extracurricular arrangement she had with his father than mutual-needs fulfilment? Was this her way of staking a claim on the business now that Laurence was gone?

She'd have to try one hell of a lot harder than that if it was.

'How touching,' he said, the bile rising in his throat, his patience at an end. 'Now, if you're quite finished?'

Her back went rigid and she stilled momentarily before reaching out her hand to Laurence's cheek one last time. Then she turned and, with barely a glance at him from her glacial blue eyes, side-stepped around Zane and slipped out of the room.

Her scent lingered in her wake, fresh and light in the clinical hospital atmosphere.

Seductive.

Irritating!

He growled his frustration out loud as he moved closer to the bed where his father lay. He was tired, he was jet-lagged and he was angry. His race halfway around the world had been for nothing; as a man who prided himself on beating every deadline thrown his way, the fact that he'd been cheated out of this one cut bone-deep.

But worse still was the realisation that, even with all that going on around him, still he could be swayed by the lingering scent of the last person he should be thinking about—his father's mistress!

'Can I give you a lift to the house?'

Ruby had been waiting outside Laurence's room the last

twenty minutes for Zane to emerge. And when he finally had, he'd pointedly ignored her and her question and headed directly to the nurses' station to talk to the medical staff.

Personally, she didn't care less where he stayed or how he got there, her only wish being that he'd turn around and disappear under whatever rock he'd been hiding under for the past decade, but Laurence's request kept pulling her back. *'Look after Zane,'* he'd implored her. And if he had been able to think fondly about a son who hadn't bothered to get in touch with him for nigh on a decade, then she could at least be civil—if only for Laurence's sake.

The staff slowly filtered away, one retrieving a bag for him from inside the nurses' station. So, he'd come direct from the airport? He'd need a lift somewhere, then. She pushed herself from the chair and tried to forget how much she disliked this man already.

'I wondered if you'd like a lift to the house?' she repeated.

He turned towards her, his features and his jaw set hard as he swung the bag up over his shoulder. The action exaggerated the broad sweep of his chest, revealing all too clearly the power in his muscled arms. Though his build was similar to his father's, he was taller and more threatening than Laurence had ever been. She felt tiny alongside him.

'I heard you.'

'And?'

'And I can take a cab.'

'That would be pointless, seeing as I'm going there, anyway.'

'Is that right?' One eyebrow arched as his eyes glinted with what looked like victory. 'And why would you be doing that?'

For just a moment she hesitated, the arrangement she'd had with Laurence and accepted as normal suddenly sending alarm bells through her. Things were going to have to change, and soon—it was one thing to share a house with Laurence, who'd been more like a father to her than a colleague; it was another thing entirely to imagine living there with his son, with his overt hostility and his latent danger. She could feel the heat rising in her cheeks as she stumbled over her answer.

'Because...I live there.'

His lip curled. A *live-in* mistress. 'How very convenient,' he said. 'My father must have enjoyed having...' *your services on tap* '...your company.'

She angled her chin higher while her eyes remained glued to his. 'Your father was a remarkable man. We shared a special friendship.'

'I'll bet,' he said dismissively. His father had a habit of forming 'special friendships'. The last one had cost Laurence the respect of his son and the complete breakdown of a father-son relationship. He was determined this one wouldn't cost him a thing.

It was only a short trip from the hospital to the house, but the BMW's air-conditioning made driving the clear winner over walking. Zane spent the brief journey staring out the windows, reacquainting himself with his old neighbourhood and trying to ignore the scent that reminded him exactly whose car and whose company he was in.

But at least she didn't talk. He had too much to assimilate right now to continue their battle of words. Already he could feel a tidal surge of bone-tiredness, the legacy of both his long journey and its unexpected conclusion, creeping up on him, numbing his senses and his mind until there were only two things he could be certain of.

His father was gone.

And life for Zane Bastiani was about to radically change.

There was little prospect it would be for the better.

Ruby steered the car into a driveway, pulling up outside the sprawling colonial bungalow that had been Zane's home for the first twenty years of his life. He uncurled himself slowly from the car, feeling a sudden and brief burst of warmth that had nothing to do with the brilliant sunlight as he took in the sight of the building.

London and his former life had never seemed so far away.

Built in the nineteen-twenties when pearl shell was gold and those who owned the pearl-lugger fleets were kings, the house was surrounded by wide verandahs and lattice fences lushly covered with flowering bougainvillea, a colourful invitation to the airy and cool interior.

The empty interior.

Bitterness seeped from a wound barely crusted over despite the passing of time. His mother had loved this house, the rambling, high-ceilinged rooms and timber floors, the large windows designed to let the slightest cooling breeze flow through. And she had loved the tropical gardens, which were always threatening to turn to jungle and overrun the house if left unchecked.

His sense of loss changed state inside him, becoming tangible, a solid thing deep in his gut. He could feel it swelling until it cramped his organs. He could taste its bitter juices in his mouth.

'Welcome home,' he muttered under his breath.

'Are you okay?'

He absorbed her words rather than heard them, just one more element to the mix of sensations and memories that reached out to snare him and drag him back into the past.

'My grandfather bought this house from one of the last of the old Master Pearlers,' he said without shifting his focus, reciting the story he'd heard so often from his mother. 'Laurence was just a kid back then. The pearl-shell industry was slowly dying and Grandfather put everything else he had in the new cultured pearl technology. He had a dream to become the first of the new breed of Master Pearlers.'

'And he made it,' she said. 'Between your grandfather and Laurence, it's quite a legacy they've left. Bastiani Pearls is now worth a fortune.'

Her words knifed through his thoughts, slicing them to ribbons, and he turned the full force of his glare on to her.

What was it with these mistresses? Anneleise could never stop thinking about money, either. Even at their last unexpected meeting, just two days before his desperate and now pointless rush to Australia, she'd staggered him by expecting some sort of compensation from him for finally getting it through her silvery blonde hair that it was over. And when he'd laughed out loud, she'd let go with the tears and lamented the opportunities she'd missed while Zane had held her undivided attention.

Even if that were anywhere near the truth, she had plenty of trinkets from their brief liaison that she could hock to tide her over if it came to that. Not that she'd take long to find another mark, if indeed she hadn't already in the time since they'd parted company. She certainly was stunning enough, with her alabaster skin and a fragile femininity that had made him want to protect her at first—until he'd discovered her fragility extended character deep. But at least now he was free of her and her parasitic tendencies. He'd had enough of grasping women, every last one of them.

'Is something wrong?' she asked, her attitude making it clear that she resented his intense scrutiny.

He turned his gaze away, pulling his bag from the boot and slamming it shut. 'Let's go inside,' he said.

Her skirt flirted around the backs of her knees as she led the way up the short set of stairs to the verandah and once again he found himself caught in the heady trail of her scent, the damnable price of chivalry.

His eyes took a moment to adjust as they entered the elegant bungalow. He looked around. The house might have been built over eighty years ago, but his mother had always seen to it that whatever renovations were made over the years had provided the most up-to-date conveniences while retaining the character of the colonial era. He let go a breath when he realised that Ruby's tenure hadn't impacted upon his mother's vision.

'I asked Kyoto to have your old room prepared in case you stayed,' she said, turning slightly towards him. 'I hope that's okay.'

He paused, not believing what he'd heard. 'Kyoto's still around?' It was inconceivable that he was still alive. The former Japanese pearl diver had worked for his family for years, first as cook and then housekeeper. He'd seemed a gnarled old man when Zane was just a boy. 'Surely he's not still working?'

She nodded, a watery smile temporarily lighting up her features. 'Mostly he supervises now—we have a cook and cleaner to do the heavy work.' He watched the wobbly smile slide away. 'But I said he should go home today. He's devastated by the news.'

She pressed her lips together and spun away, turning her back on him, but not before he'd recognised the crack in her voice, the slight tremulous quality to her movements as she'd uttered that last word that told him she was either trying very hard not to cry or, if Anneleise was any guide, trying her best to make him think she was. Anneleise could have written a thesis on the artful use of tears—although he doubted she'd ever shed a sincere one in her life. Why wouldn't Ruby be armed with the same arsenal? It probably came with the job description.

'Well,' she murmured, her back still to him, her voice low and strained as she rubbed her brow with one hand, 'I'm sure you don't need me to show you where your room is. I'll leave you to settle in.'

He could just walk away, keep walking down the passageway to his old room. He could just ignore her and let her know her ploy had left him completely unmoved. He *should* just walk away.

But the urge to show her that he wouldn't fall for her tricks was too great. She needed to know that he knew all about the games women liked to play when there was money at stake. She needed to know that he wouldn't be falling for any of them.

He reached a hand to her shoulder, ignoring her startled flinch at his grip as he steered her around to face him.

He overcame her resistance, tipping up her stiffly held jaw with one hand until there was no way she could avoid his gaze any longer. Slowly, reluctantly, her eyes slid upwards, until their aqua depths collided with his. In the first instant he took in the moisture, the lashes damp and dark, and he had to acknowledge she was good, very good, if she could bring on the tears that readily.

But then he saw what was inside her eyes and it slashed him to the core.

Pain. Loss. Mind-numbing desolation.

All of those things he recognised. All of those things found an echo in a place deep down inside himself, something that shifted and ached afresh as her liquid eyes seemed to bare her soul to him. It was an awkward feeling, uncomfortable, unwelcome.

He watched as she jammed her lips together as a solitary tear squeezed from the corner of one eye. Momentarily disarmed, acting purely on instinct, he shifted his hand from her chin and gently wiped the tear from her cheek with the pad of one finger. Her eyelids dipped shut, her lips parted as she drew in a sudden breath, and he felt her tremble into his touch.

Gears crunched and ground together inside him. This wasn't going the way he'd expected at all. Because *she* wasn't the way he'd expected.

'You really cared about him?'

The question betrayed his thoughts, clumsy and heavily weighted with disbelief. But there was no time to correct it— the thought that Laurence meant more to her than a mere provider of luxury and cash somehow grated hard on his senses.

She dragged in a breath and pulled away, shrugging off his hand as she backed into a cane lounge. 'Is that so hard to believe? Laurence made it easy to want to care about him.'

Her rapid admission changed everything, transforming his confused thoughts into sizzling hot anger in an instant as the facts slotted back into their rightful place. Laurence had *'made it easy'*. No pretence, no circumspection. She'd admitted how it had been between them with barely a blink! And it was exactly what he'd expected. No wonder she felt so crushed. She'd lost her sugar daddy along with her cash flow.

'Yeah. I'll just *bet* he made it easy.'

She edged closer, her head tilted, as if she couldn't have heard him right. 'I'm not sure I understand you. What exactly do you mean?'

'It's hardly that difficult to work out. A rich old man with a taste for pretty women and who could afford to make having one around worth her while.'

If he hadn't been jet-lagged, if he hadn't been awake throughout too many flights over too many time zones, maybe he would have had a chance of fending off her next attack. As it was, he didn't see it coming.

Her flattened palm cracked against his cheek and jaw like a bullet from a gun.

Instantly she recoiled in horror, her eyes wide open, the offending hand fisted over her mouth. She waited while he drew in a long breath and rubbed the place she'd made contact, the skin under his hand already a slash of colour. But he didn't react, not physically, and she felt the shock ebb away, felt her panicked heart rate calm just enough to match the simmer of anger that still consumed her.

'Well, you sure pack a punch,' he drawled, working his jaw from side to side, his eyes narrow and hard like he was assessing her all over again.

'Nothing more than you deserved.' He'd asked for it all right. Why would he think that about Laurence? Why would he think that about *her*? 'And don't think I'm going to apologise. I don't have to take that kind of garbage from you.'

'Because you can't handle the truth?'

'You're unbelievable! You really believe I'm here for Laurence's money?'

'Most people would be lured by it.'

'Then I'm not "most people". I don't want his money. I never have.'

'Then why else would you have been living with him, a man old enough to have been your father?'

She laughed then, mostly because she knew that if she didn't laugh, she'd probably cry with the injustice of it all. He was so wrong. He didn't know his father. He didn't know her. *He knew nothing.*

'I pity you,' she said, much more calmly than she felt. 'Obviously you're completely unfamiliar with the words "friendship" or "companionship".'

He snorted his disbelief and her anger escalated to dangerous levels again. But this time she was determined to keep control. She had to try to remember what Laurence had asked of her. She dragged in a deep breath, battling to stay rational and calm, in spite of his attack.

'Just because you were incapable of showing your father any respect or affection...' she shook her head '...don't assume everybody else was.'

His eyes narrowed dangerously, the resentment contained within so hard and absolute, it glistened. 'So you looked after him out of the goodness of your heart? You stayed merely to keep him company? Next you'll be expecting me to believe you really loved him.'

'*Somebody* had to! God only knows he got nothing but grief from you.'

She jerked herself away, wanting to get out of there, wanting to get as far away from him as she could, but a steel grip on her arm stopped her dead, preventing her escape. She turned, indignant, but the protest died on her lips the moment she saw his face, his features contorted with fury.

'Don't you try to take the high moral ground with me. You have *no idea* what I felt for my father or why. None at all.'

She fisted her hand and wrenched at her arm unsuccessfully. So instead she leaned closer, so close she could feel the anger coming out of him like heat from an open fire. But his anger was nothing compared to hers—she was angry enough for both of them.

'You're right,' she agreed, feeling her lip curl in contempt. 'I have no idea what you felt or why. But whose fault is that? Mine, for being here when your father needed support, or yours, for not caring enough to be here yourself?'

CHAPTER THREE

HOURS LATER, as the first unlayering of the night sky heralded the coming dawn, Zane had given up on sleep. He lay on his bed in the room that had been his for more than half his life, the accumulated photographs and trophies from his youth still exactly where he'd left them. If he closed his eyes, he could almost imagine he'd never left. But he knew he wouldn't be thinking about how things used to be. Because the last few hours had shown him that all he'd be thinking about was a woman with fire in her eyes and venom on her tongue, a woman built like a goddess and who fought like a she-cat.

Even last night, when she'd lashed out and slapped him, she hadn't backed away. She'd come back for more and she'd given more. And even when she'd agreed with him, in their final exchange, she'd hit back with such a sting in her parting comments that when she'd yanked her arm against his grip once more he'd had no choice but to let her go.

She had some spirit. He wrestled once more with the sheets as he tried to get comfortable. What would she be like in bed? He'd lay odds that she'd show as much life out of her clothes, if not more, than she did in them.

He punched his pillow one final time before giving up, swinging his legs off the bed and making for the *en suite*, dragging his hands over his troubled head. What the hell was wrong with him? It didn't matter what she was like in bed, he was hardly about to pick up where his father left off!

Besides, he had more pressing problems to turn his mind to now. There would be all kinds of things to deal with: a funeral to arrange, the future of the business. Naturally he'd be expected to fill Laurence's shoes for the time being, but plans would have to be made for the longer term. He might as well make a start on it before Ruby could interfere. She might have held a high place in Laurence's 'affections', but, now he was here, things were going to change.

Kyoto was waiting for him in the kitchen when he emerged, finally feeling more human after a long hot shower and fresh clothes.

'Mister Zane!' Kyoto shouted in welcome as he approached, his wrinkled face contorted between half-toothless smile, half anguish. 'It's so good you're home. I make you breakfast, "special".'

Sinewy arms suddenly wrapped tightly around him in a rapid embrace before releasing him just as quickly and returning to the task of scrambling eggs as if they'd never touched him. Zane smiled to himself. Kyoto's broken English was just the same, but he could never remember a time when he'd ever been so physically demonstrative. It was strangely touching.

'It's good to see you again, too,' he said sincerely.

'Your father,' Kyoto said, shaking his head as he heaped a plate full. 'I am so sorry.'

'Thank you,' he said, right now feeling Kyoto's loss more than his own, as hot coffee and a heavily laden breakfast plate with a stack of toast on the side was placed in front of him.

Kyoto disappeared, muttering sadly to himself as Zane made a start on breakfast in the large, airy room. It was hours since his last real meal and Kyoto's cooking had never been a hardship to endure, least of all now. He'd almost made his way through the mountain when Kyoto returned and something else appeared on the table before him. He blinked in cold hard shock as he recognised the small padlocked wooden chest.

The old pearler skipper's box had always sat in pride of place on his father's desk and now it sat in front of him, bold and challenging. *Mocking*.

A relic of a former era, when natural pearls were real treasure and the rare bonus discovered while collecting the mother-of-pearl shell itself, any such pearls were deposited through a small hole in the lid and so kept secure during the lugger's time at sea.

But it was hardly pearls he knew the box contained. More like dynamite.

'Your father said you were to have,' Kyoto said in response to Zane's unspoken question.

Zane set his plate aside and drained the last of his strong coffee, never taking his eyes off the chest. The wood had aged to an even richer golden patina than he remembered, the metal handle and lock scratched and scarred by the passage of time, the tiny key clearly in place. Inviting. Taunting. Because it was hardly the chest his father wanted him to have. It was the contents. And Zane knew exactly what was inside.

Did his father honestly not realise Zane knew, or was he merely trying to press the point home—a bitter reminder of the circumstances of his leaving? No question, Zane decided. Of course he would have known. Clearly his father hadn't asked to see Zane in order to settle their differences. He'd called for him to rub them in!

His mind rankled with the stench of the fetid memories. He'd been just a young boy home on school holidays when he'd sneaked into his father's office under the cool verandah and had been exploring through the desk drawers until he'd come across a small battered key. Instantly he'd thought of the box on top of the desk, the box that had been locked as long as he could remember and which had always intrigued him. So he'd scrabbled up on to his father's wide jarrah desk and tested the lock. It had clicked open on the second scratchy attempt. With a thrill of discovery he'd removed the lock and the metal plate from the catch. He remembered holding his breath as he'd lifted the lid to peer at whatever treasures lay inside.

And he remembered the crush of disappointment when he'd found it only contained a stash of old letters. Barely half-interested by then, he'd picked the first from the top of the pile. He'd opened the folded sheet, only to stare at a letter from his father to his so-called Aunt Bonnie, his mother's best friend. There was a list of numbers and something about a house and a monthly payment that made no sense at all to his young mind. But there'd been no time to linger over it once his nanny had discovered him in the room he'd been forbidden to enter and warned him never to look in places he shouldn't in case he learned something he never wanted or needed to know.

For a while he'd wondered what she'd meant but then he'd found a new game to play and gone back to school and he'd forgotten all about it. Until that day, nine stark years ago, when he'd been reminded of the letter and its contents and suddenly it had all made perfect sense!

He heaved a sigh as he considered the box, the stain of bitterness deep and permanent in his mind. What was his father really playing at, leaving him the box like this? Did he expect him to read the entire contents—no doubt their love letters—making sure Zane knew the whole sordid truth? Was this all Laurence thought Zane deserved after walking out nine years before? Was this to be his inheritance? Zane couldn't help but raise a smile ironically as he contemplated the box. He wouldn't put it past him. His father had never been known for his subtlety.

But he wasn't playing into that game. He'd read enough all those years ago to last him. The box could stay closed.

Kyoto whisked away his plates and swept around the kitchen, cleaning everything he touched until it gleamed.

'More coffee?' he offered, interrupting Zane's thoughts.

Zane responded with a shake of the head, giving the box a final push away as he stood. He didn't need any reminders of the past. He had Ruby to do that.

'Thank you, Kyoto, but no. I need to get started on a few things. Is there a car I can use while I'm here?'

'Yes, yes.' He nodded. 'But you are home to stay now, for good?'

Zane dragged in a breath. His immediate plans for the company included making the long-term arrangements that would ensure his speedy return to London and his businesses there. Of course, there would be ramifications of his father's sudden death to deal with—someone would have to take over the running of the pearl business; he'd source a manager somehow—but staying wasn't an option right now. 'We'll see, Kyoto,' he replied noncommittally. 'First, I just need to make sure the company gets through this difficult stage, without my father's hand to guide it.'

'Not a problem,' Kyoto offered, waving away his concerns with a flick of his tea towel. 'Miss Ruby take care of all that, no worry.'

Zane stilled, a knife-sharp feeling of foreboding slicing through his thoughts. 'What do you mean?'

'Miss Ruby already at the office. She take care of everything.'

* * *

If indigestion came in a colour, it would be red. If it came in the shape of a woman, it would take the form of Ruby Clemenger.

She sat now in his father's office, behind his father's desk, like she owned it, making notes on a laptop computer as she studied an open file on the desk.

'You haven't wasted a minute, I see,' he said, announcing his presence in the same sentence.

She looked up, momentarily startled, before the shutters clamped down on her eyes again, turning them frosty blue. Guarded.

'I expected you'd sleep longer.'

He smiled. 'So you thought you'd get a head start on running the company before I woke up?'

She frowned. 'And why would you possibly think that?'

He gestured around the spacious office. 'Because you're here, barely twenty-four hours after my father's death, in *his* office, occupying *his* desk.'

She put down her pen and leaned back in her chair—*his father's chair*—her eyes narrowing to icy blue channels. 'Is that what you're worried about? That I might want to take your precious birthright away from you? That I might steal your inheritance and whisk Bastiani Pearls away from you while you're not looking?'

'You wouldn't stand a chance!' He squeezed the words through lips dragged tight, his jaw held rigid.

She smiled, a smile that exposed her even white teeth but extended no further. 'Then maybe it's just as well I'm not interested.'

'So how do you explain being here now?' he demanded, moving closer to the broad desk. 'It's Saturday. Not exactly office hours.'

I had to get out of the house, she thought. *I had to get away from you.* But she wouldn't say it. Didn't want to admit the blatant honesty of her thoughts, even to herself. Instead she steeled herself against his approach and said, 'I have work to do. Laurence and I were involved in a project together last week when he took ill. The file was still on his desk. And I really didn't think he'd mind me borrowing his office for a while.'

'What kind of work?' he demanded, shrugging off her sarcasm like he expected it.

She surveyed him as he made his way around the desk to her side, taking in the cool-looking chinos and fine-knit shirt, resenting every lean stride he took closer to her. He was dressed for the heat, so why was it that her temperature was suddenly rising?

Damn the man! She'd told herself all night—she'd *promised* herself—that now they'd got their first meeting out of the way, now that they both knew where they stood with each other, that she'd be immune to his power and his sheer masculine force. And finally she'd convinced herself that that would be the case, that she could wear her anger like steel plating around her. But she'd been kidding herself. Otherwise, why else would she have fled the house at first light? And why else would she be feeling the encroaching heat of this man like the kiss of a blowtorch?

Her anger was still there, and the resentment—with just one comment, he'd managed to resurrect that in spades—but there was no avoiding the Bastiani aura.

Like father, like son.

Laurence's power had made him a powerful colleague to work with, a fascinating and inspiring mentor. Zane, though, seemed to take the family trait to a new level, his proximity grating on her resistance, his raw masculine magnetism and fresh man-scent leaving her feeling strangely vulnerable.

'What are these?' he asked, looking down at the drawings on the desk, breaking her out of her reflections.

'The new range,' she said, feeling a note of pride creep into her voice as he sorted through the designs she'd been working on for over six months. 'We've called them the Passion Collection. The launch is a little over three months away.'

'Here?'

'Like all our collections, we'll launch in Broome first, at the Stairway to the Moon festival, then we'll take the collection nationwide with an event at the Sydney Opera House one week later. We'll follow that up with the dealer visits, where we take selected designs to New York and London. No doubt you'll expect to come along, in Laurence's place.'

She tried to infuse some kind of welcome note to her voice, but if he was impressed by the demanding launch schedule or wanted any part of it, he didn't show it. 'These designs are very ambitious,' he said instead. 'Extraordinarily so.'

'Thank you.'

He looked around sharply. 'These are yours?'

She nodded. *Every last one of them.* 'That is why I was employed here,' she told him, holding his gaze. 'I design settings for the pearls the Bastiani Corporation produces.'

'Then you must realise that wasn't exactly a compliment. These designs will never work.'

She stilled, not believing what she was hearing. 'I beg your pardon?'

'These designs—"The Passion Collection": *A Lovers' Embrace.* It's a fine concept, but don't you think it's too ambitious to achieve with just pearls and gold and gemstones? You'll never pull it off. We can't have an entire collection based around such a crazy idea. It's too much of a risk.'

'It *will* work,' she argued, trying to banish the doubt demons that assailed her creative mind at every opportunity without Zane's input to spur them on. 'Yes, it's ambitious, and, yes, it's a risk, but it's already in production. *And* it's almost complete.'

'But not finished and not proven. So the Bastiani Corporation is pinning its future hopes on a collection that could be a major failure?'

'Laurence was passionate about this collection. He was behind it one hundred percent.'

'Laurence isn't here now.'

'But *I* am. And I've been designing pearl collections for Bastiani ever since I started working here—so far very successfully. There's no reason to think this one won't be as successful.'

He put down the drawing he'd been holding and swivelled, leaning back against the desk, his hands poised either side of his legs. 'You'd hardly claim anything else.'

He was too close. Dealing with him while he'd had his back to her was one thing, having him staring her down while hovering alongside was something else. It made her wish she'd pulled on a whole lot more this morning than a floral wrap skirt and a cool, lemon-coloured singlet top. She pushed herself out of her chair, using the pretext of filling her water glass at the cooler, and only turned when she'd taken three steadying breaths.

'Well, I don't intend to let Laurence or the company down now,' she said, in a bid to regain her composure. 'And while we're on the topic, did you ever bother to read those financial reports I know your father had sent to you regularly?' she asked. 'Did you ever take note of what they told you, and of how the profits of the Bastiani Corporation took off exponentially, when instead of selling cultured pearl stocks and basic design elements, we started selling themed collections twice a year?'

'And you're claiming the credit for that, I presume?' He practically snorted the words out, without bothering to make any attempt to answer her question.

'No,' she said, shaking her head. 'I'm not claiming the credit.

Laurence took me on as a junior designer when I was barely out of design school. He said he wanted someone fresh, with no preconceived or outmoded ideas of how pearl jewellery should look. So together we worked on the idea of a themed collection, an entire range that would display the beauty and mystique of the most magnificent and highly prized pearls in the world. So, it was Laurence who had the vision, who had the dream of expanding his business in a way the company had never done before. But the designs were all mine.'

She stopped, feeling suddenly heady, as if oxygen was in short supply. All through her impassioned speech he'd sat, coolly surveying her from his position against the desk, his eyes hooded, almost slumberous.

If she didn't like his attitude, she resented his silent scrutiny even more. In desperation, she took a sip from the glass, trying to fill the space in the conversation, suddenly glad she'd had the foresight to fill her glass now that her mouth and lips had turned desert dry. Condensation beaded as she tilted the glass, running down the side, making tiny rivulets around her fingers. She gasped as two icy drops splashed on to her singlet, leaching into the light fabric in ever-expanding circles.

His eyes followed the movement. He'd been fascinated watching her retreat, seeing her calm herself before facing him and stating her case. He'd been impressed by her no-nonsense sense of her own worth in the company—in spite of himself.

But right now he was more impressed with the way the droplets of water were soaking tantalisingly into the fabric of her top. He liked what it did to rattle her composure. He liked even better what it did to her breasts. In an instant they'd firmed and peaked and, like an invitation he couldn't refuse, he was drawn closer.

'You're turning out to be a woman of considerable talents,' he murmured, as he bridged the few steps between them. He came to a halt immediately before her. She was tall enough, but still she had to turn her head up to look him in the eye. That was good—that gave him an uninterrupted view of the sweep of her throat and the swell of tanned-to-honey-gold skin that disappeared tantalisingly under her singlet top.

She swallowed as he reached out a hand between them, her eyes wide like a startled doe's, fearful and uncertain. He put his fingers to the pearl choker at her throat, lifting it gently from her satin smooth skin, feeling the pearl's warmth where it had lain against her flesh.

'And is this one of yours, too?'

She couldn't breathe, she couldn't move, as a fear she hadn't felt in a long time resurfaced, threatening to swamp her. *Danger*, she recognised. The man meant danger. He was way too close, way too imposing and when he'd reached out a hand she'd thought— Oh, Lord, just the way he'd been watching her breasts had felt like the graze of a man's hand. And if his gaze could be that powerful... If he'd reached out to touch her there...

But instead he'd picked up her choker, the trace of his fingertips against her throat a tingling trail, searingly heated, shockingly intimate. She shuddered under his touch, a rush of realisation, some sixth sense alerting her that this danger was like nothing she'd known before. This brand of danger was more potent, more powerful and much more magnetic.

'It's beautiful,' he said, his voice husky and low and further tugging on her senses as he examined the piece. 'Just like its wearer.' His eyes lifted till they met hers. 'Did you design it?'

Breath rushed into the vacuum of her lungs. But she couldn't let herself reflect on what he'd just said, even though his rich dark eyes seemed intent on making her forget everything else. She had to concentrate on the necklace—and on what he'd asked.

It shouldn't be so hard, not to talk about one of her favourite pieces. Suspended on a band of nitrite, the single gem was held in place by an intricate coil of gold. The pearl, a magnificent eighteen-millimetre perfect round, had been a gift from Laurence following the success of their first collection. It had seemed appropriate that she should wear it today.

'I made it,' she admitted at last, reaching up to her neck instinctively, only to encounter his hand still cradling the piece. For a second their fingers brushed and lingered—and she saw something fleeting skid across his eyes, a spark, a surge of flame, and a corresponding heat pooled low in her belly.

'That's some pearl,' he murmured without letting go, his eyes now on her lips and not on the pearl at all. But there was no time to consider why that should be so, not with his mouth hovering near, the subtle tugging pressure he was exerting on her choker drawing her closer.

She swallowed, tried to make her mouth work, her senses filled with the scent of him, warm and woody and wanting her.

'Thank you,' she whispered, already imagining the taste of his lips on hers, already liking it. 'Laurence gave it to me.'

He blinked, his eyes changing from caramel warm to granite cold in an instant. Then he dropped the choker and straightened.

'No doubt you made it worth his while.'

The mood shattered, with her thoughts in total disarray. This time when her fingers found her pearl they circled the precious gem like it was a talisman, praying for it to give her strength. But she would need more than a pearl if she intended to keep this man at bay.

So she gathered her thoughts and bit back, 'Oh, yes. I'd certainly like to think so.'

Anger lit the eyes filled so recently with desire. *Anger and disgust.*

'Tell me it's not true,' he demanded. 'Tell me you didn't sleep with my father.'

She stared up at him and allowed herself a half-smile. So he wasn't disgusted with her? He was disgusted with himself, disgusted that he could be attracted to someone his father had slept with. Maybe Laurence's gift would protect her after all, because as long as Zane saw her as the pearl master's mistress, she would be safe from him. And, more importantly, she would be safe from her own quavering resistance.

'I don't have to tell you anything! It's none of your business.' She moved to go around him and return to her desk, but his hands grabbed hold of her shoulders, dragging her in, imprisoning her close to him.

'Did you?'

She looked down at his hands. 'I'm surprised you can even bear to touch me.' Then she focused her gaze until it was needle sharp and hitched one eyebrow provocatively. 'Or are you merely intent on ensuring you inherit *all* your father's assets?'

She didn't wait for his response. She shrugged off his hands and marched to the desk, collecting up her designs and plans. 'Excuse me, I'd love to stay and chat, but I have work to do. And then I'm going home—to pack.'

'Why? Where are you going?'

'I don't know,' she admitted halfway across the room. 'But it's going to be bad enough working with you until the launch. There's just no way I can stomach the thought of living with you, as well.'

'What do you mean,' he called out behind her, '"until the launch"?'

She dragged in a breath and slowly swivelled around, sending up a silent apology to Laurence as she did so. But it wasn't so much that she wouldn't honour his deathbed request, she told herself, she was merely putting a time limit on it.

'I'm giving my notice, Zane. I'll stay until the launch of

the new collection. I'll finish what I have to do. But then you won't have to put up with me any more. I'll be leaving Broome—for good.'

CHAPTER FOUR

LAURENCE HAD CLEARLY had other ideas. A few days later both Ruby and Zane sat dumbfounded in Laurence's former office as his executor explained the terms of his will.

'I don't understand,' Ruby said uncertainly. But it wasn't that she hadn't heard the lawyer the first time; it was just that it made no sense.

Derek Finlayson breathed an apologetic sigh. 'I realise it's a lot to take in right now, but basically what it comes down to is that you and Zane have been bequeathed equal shares in ninety per cent of the Bastiani Pearl Corporation. As of now you each control forty-five per cent of the business.'

'But…' She looked around for help, but Zane wasn't giving any. He sat, rigid and fixed, his face a tight mask. 'But I don't want it.'

Zane swung his head around, the disbelief in his features reading like an accusation.

She shook her head. Nothing made sense. Just last weekend she'd moved her things out of the house and into a cabin at the Cable Beach Resort. It was five-star luxury all the way, but that wasn't the reason she'd chosen it. It was because it was about as far away as she could possibly get from Zane. And she'd figured it would only be for the short term. Already

she had some interviews lined up with jewellery manu-
facturers in Sydney. In the past few years, she'd made herself
a solid reputation with the Bastiani Corporation. The successful launch of the Passion Collection would seal it. If all went
well, she'd be on her way out of Broome in just a matter of
months.

But if she stayed...

She couldn't let herself think about what that would be like.
Right now she knew she'd be gone from Zane and his
poisoned atmosphere in less than three months. She couldn't
bear to think about what it would be like to have to survive
any longer than that.

'I *don't* want it,' she insisted, her throat squeezed tight. 'I
don't understand why Laurence would have done this at all. In
fact, I've already started making arrangements to leave Broome
for good. I have job prospects. I won't even be here—'

The solicitor removed his glasses and rubbed the crinkled
bridge of his nose and looked like he was about to say something, before he stopped suddenly, as if thinking better of it.
Instead, he gave a measured sigh and replaced the glasses,
peering intently through them down the long sweep of his
nose at her. 'Clearly, under the terms of the will,' he started,
his words delivered slowly for more effect, 'Laurence
expected you to remain here in Broome to co-manage the corporation with Zane. Maybe you might want to take a moment
to reconsider your position? The remaining ten per cent of the
business will be apportioned among the employees and house
staff based on length of service to the company. They will
need the business run profitably for their benefit, as well.'

'Let her go,' Zane interrupted. 'She doesn't want to stay!
I'll buy her out.'

Derek Finlayson blinked and directed his grey steely gaze
towards Zane. 'I understand your distress, Mr Bastiani, but

it's your father's wishes that I'm concerned with right now. Laurence clearly wished for both you and Miss Clemenger to manage the business for the benefit of *all* the stakeholders. But, after all, it's been Miss Clemenger who's been working alongside Laurence for several years now. Right now she would be more familiar with the actual business. It's crucial she stays, you must see that.'

'I haven't exactly been sitting on my hands, myself. I have businesses of my own to take care of in London.'

'Your father provided for that,' said the lawyer, riffling through his notes, letting the acid in Zane's comment slide by. 'Ah, yes, here it is. You'll have whatever time you need to return to London and do a handover. I can run you through the details later.

'Now, Miss Clemenger,' he continued, 'Laurence clearly knew how you felt about looking after the business and the employees. And he trusted you to champion those rights and to carry on his vision—to keep the Bastiani Corporation at the forefront of the industry in both pearl design and innovation. He trusted you to look after the company's profitability for not only your benefit, but for theirs, as well. Is there anything else I can say that will help convince you?'

'But if she doesn't want to stay—'

'No!' Ruby wheeled her head around, blue eyes clashing with seething brown. 'Mr Finlayson is right. Laurence wanted this. He wanted me to stay. I'm not about to walk away from my responsibility to the business or to the employees. And there's just no way I'm going to let Laurence down!'

Derek Finlayson's lips pulled into an unfamiliar smile as he pounded the table with his fist. 'That's the ticket! Laurence would be proud of you, my dear. As for you, Zane, how long do you think you'll need to hand over your businesses? That is…' He regarded him through shrewd eyes, his eyebrows arched '…if you *do* intend to return to Broome to co-manage the business?'

'Oh, I'll be back,' he said, looking at Ruby, his hostile eyes incinerating the air between them. 'Make no mistake about that.'

'How did you manage that?'

The lawyer had gone, the room was empty of everyone except her and Zane, yet the atmosphere still felt too crowded, too thick with tension, too thunderous with his snapped words.

Her mind a whirl, Ruby barely registered his question over her own panicked second thoughts. *She was trapped.* She'd been so close to walking away, just twelve short weeks away from being free, and now she was locked into the Bastiani Corporation, effectively shackled to a man she despised. *Shackled by pearls.* Had Laurence had any concept of what he'd done to her?

"Look after Zane," his father had begged. She wanted to laugh. From what she'd seen, Zane needed nobody to look after him. But she'd look after the company, she had no problem with that. But as for Zane, Zane could look after himself.

'What an extraordinary coup.'

'What do you mean?' She responded absently as his words finally filtered through, more intrigued right now that he saw things so differently to her. Why on earth would he think this was what she wanted? The concept that she was now suddenly worth a very large fortune, in addition to what her own family connections provided her with, was no compensation for her growing fears.

Laurence had done her no favours.

This was no beneficial bequest.

This was a sentence.

'It's not like you're family. You're merely an employee. So

how did you manage to convince my father to leave you forty-five per cent of the company?'

She dragged her eyes away from the bookshelves she'd been staring through and looked up at him, trying to blink away her confusion.

'I did nothing to "*convince*" him. I had no idea your father decided to frame his will that way. Why would I?'

'No idea?' He snorted his disbelief. 'You lived with him and you make out you didn't know? Surely you can understand that's just a little difficult to believe.'

She shook her head. 'Of course I didn't know! I told you I was resigning. You knew I was leaving. Why would I have made those plans if I'd known anything about Laurence's bequest?'

'Don't play the innocent. You never had any intention of leaving! Not while you had a chance of benefiting in my father's will. Saying you'd stay till the launch safely covered you there.'

She sighed, raising both her hands to the ceiling. What was the point of trying to convince him? What did it matter what he thought? 'It doesn't matter what you believe,' she acceded. 'The fact is, Laurence has given me no choice. I have no option but to stay.'

He laughed, harsh and bitter, seizing on her admission. 'Funny how quickly a few hundred million dollars can make you change your tune. Of course,' he mocked, disbelief dripping from his words, 'we know it's not really the money.'

'I *don't* care about the money! Not for me. But if I leave, what happens to the employees? You'll be gone for how long? Who would manage the company? How is that going to carry on Laurence's vision? I can't do that to people I worked with, that Laurence wanted to be looked after. I can't do that to people like Kyoto, after all his years of service.'

'You'll stay for the sake of the employees? How noble of you.' He leaned up close. 'Pardon me if I don't believe there isn't just a smattering of self-interest involved.'

'No pardon necessary,' she hissed back. 'I wouldn't expect you to believe anything, let alone the truth. You've shown a marked absence of that ability ever since you arrived back in Broome.'

'And you've shown a remarkable *inability* to admit to the truth! Why do you pretend to be something you're not? Why do you pretend not to understand what is so obvious to everyone else?'

She put her hands on her hips. Damn the man for his constant slurs and sordid innuendoes. 'So what is it that's so obvious to everyone else, Zane? What exactly do you mean? Maybe you should get it right off your chest.'

'You need it spelt out? Okay! Why the hell would my father leave you such a huge share of the company? Forty-five per cent! You've already admitted my father was special to you. So why would he leave you a fortune if you weren't something very much more than special?'

A rush of blood surged and crashed in her ears, urging her to fight.

'You're saying your father settled a fortune on me for living with him—for being his mistress. Is that right?'

'Got it in one.'

'Why is it with you that everything has to come down to sex?'

'Doesn't it?'

She wanted to disagree, but then, wasn't this exactly what she wanted him to think? If he hated her for sleeping with his father, then he wouldn't want to touch her, and if he didn't touch her, then she'd have a chance of resisting this bizarre magnetism of his, she'd have a chance of not falling victim to his power.

So instead of giving in to the inciting jungle beat of her heart and lashing back a reply in the negative, she embarked on a different course. Arching one eyebrow provocatively, she pasted on a sultry smile and pushed her chest out conspicuously. He liked her breasts, he'd already made that more than clear. And then, as if on cue, his eyes followed the movements of her bustline, his gaze hot and hungry, and her smile widened. She knew she was baiting him, but it was no more than he deserved. He'd already made his mind up about her and it suited her purposes. Why not go with his prejudices? Why not play them for all they were worth?

'Well, you've sure got me there, Zane,' she said, her voice intentionally husky as she ran one hand slowly down the curve of her hip. 'You *know* damn well I was special to him. Obviously our relationship meant a lot more to him than I realised. I never expected him to be quite so generous in return.'

The scarlet hue to his skin deepened as his throat corded and kicked out a pulse.

'You know,' she said in mock understanding, placing a flirty finger along her cheek as her tactics bore such luscious fruit. 'I know what your problem is. I suspect maybe I was even more special to him than his own son. That's what really gets your back up, isn't it Zane? He loved me, and not you. That's what you can't abide. That's why you hate me so much, isn't it?'

He propelled himself a step closer, his movements charged with super-anger, his features contorted with rage, and Ruby's heart skipped a beat. Why was he so angry when she was merely agreeing with whatever tawdry views of her he already held? His enraged features told her she'd more than made her mark—she'd gone too far!

'Zane…' she uttered, taking an instinctive step backwards as he powered closer. 'I didn't mean—'

The pulse in his brow hammered visibly, his eyes wild with turmoil, and whatever she'd been going to say was forgotten in the broiling atmosphere.

'Of course he loved you more than he loved me. Why wouldn't he want to?' he said, his voice strangely soft, at odds with his entire posture. He reached out a hand and she could see the tension in his corded muscles, his tight skin. She flinched, but his hand moved to one side, to touch her hair, to softly curl a loose strand around his finger, to curve the back of his hand over her cheek as his eyes travelled over her face, burning a trail down to her shoulders, her bustline. Then lower....

She swallowed. 'No,' she whispered, sensing the danger had shifted gears and taken a new direction—a new direction that had her body humming with interest instead of shrinking away in fear. She licked her lips, her breathing suddenly shallow and unreliable as if he'd burned up the oxygen between them. 'I didn't mean that. I was wrong—'

He hushed her mouth with a finger from his other hand, stopping her words and her breath in the same instant. His scent wound its way into her, his taste leached into her recently moistened lips and his touch was so tender. So tender when he should be so angry.

She didn't want him to be tender. She wanted him angry. Angry was consistent. Angry she could deal with. But this sudden tenderness...

Somehow this was infinitely more dangerous.

'You *were* right,' he admitted at last, dropping the hand at her mouth to skim down her throat and over the fullness of her breasts like an electric charge that made her gasp involuntarily as it scorched a trail all the way down. 'You obviously gave him something I never could. But I have to ask myself one question. For a forty-five per cent share in the company, for something like two hundred million dollars—'

He hesitated, his face just a hair's breadth away from her, his pause like a vacuum between them while his heated gaze continued to read her eyes, to caress her lips, as brazen as a torch brand on her flesh while the gentle pressure on her hair kept her close. And then his head tilted as his lips curled up into a thin, contemptible smile.

'Well, it sure begs the question—just how good *are* you in bed?'

CHAPTER FIVE

LIKE A GUNSLINGER'S trigger finger, her hand itched to let fly. His face was temptingly close and already she knew how satisfying it could be to crack her open palm against that arrogant visage. But too often lately with this man she'd let her emotions rule her actions and she'd lashed out either verbally or physically, only to immediately regret her lack of control. She wouldn't let herself give in to that base instinct again, no matter what the provocation.

Instead, she jammed her fingers into a tight knot behind her back and forced out a laugh even while her nails dug sharply into the flesh of her palms.

'I wouldn't give that a second thought,' she said, flicking her head away, yanking the curl of her hair from his reach. 'Because that's the one thing you'll *never* find out.'

Triumph fizzed in her veins as she turned for the door. She'd done it! She'd kept her cool *and* put him well and truly in his place.

He watched her stride away, her chin thrust high as if she'd just won some major battle, even though her movements still looked wobbly, almost as if she was having a hard time making the transformation from warm and soft to cold and aloof. And she had been only too warm and soft and alive a moment ago. He'd felt her sculpted perfection under the glance of his hand. He'd sensed her feminine power. She was magnificent when she was enraged, and yet with a vulnerability that cracked any hard edges right off.

No wonder his father had fallen so hard. He suppressed a growl. He didn't want to think about her with his father! To throw herself away on someone like him—*what a waste*!

But if she'd thought she'd got away with the last word— bad luck.

'My father always was a sucker for a bit on the side,' he reminded her, 'but for all the millions you've been gifted, I sincerely hope he got enough *bang for his buck.*'

Her eyes blazed with fury in a face flushed with rage. *'How dare you!'* she fired, wheeling her body around to confront him, her stance aggressive, ready to fight. 'You can say or think what you like about me—I don't care!—but I will *not* stand by and hear you denigrate your father's memory. What kind of son are you that you can say such things when Laurence is barely cold in his grave? Your father was a man of integrity—not that you'd have any concept what that means!'

His eyebrows rose of their own accord. So she still had fight? He had to hand it to her, she didn't give up easily. But then, given the right financial incentive, she'd soon buckle.

'Trust me,' he assured her, as he leaned back lazily against the desk. 'I know more about my father than you give me credit for.'

She laughed. 'I'd sooner put my trust in a crocodile!'

'Come, now, Ruby,' he soothed, setting his voice to bored reasonableness. 'You know you don't have to defend my father any more. So drop the act. You've got your reward. Why not take it?'

'What? You seriously think I consider Laurence's bizarre bequest as some kind of *reward*? By forcing me to work alongside you? A prison sentence would be more appealing right now.'

He pushed himself away from the desk towards her. 'For once, I couldn't agree more.'

Her eyes narrowed as he moved closer, as if surprised by his ready agreement, her body becoming more erect, more defiant with each step he took.

'Clearly neither of us wants to have anything to do with the other. So I have the perfect solution.' He smiled. 'I'll buy you out. I'll pay for your share of the company with cold hard cash. You can be out of Broome on the first available flight. Out of here and able to take advantage of those job opportunities you've got lined up elsewhere. Not that you'll need a job ever again with what you'll walk away with.'

Oh, yes, the idea definitely held appeal for her, he could tell by the tilt of her head, the hope in her eyes. Was she working out her price? Without a doubt.

'The lawyer said—'

'Whatever the lawyer said is irrelevant,' he argued with a swipe of his hand for emphasis. 'This is between you and me. We're the major shareholders now. What we decide goes.'

'And the launch?'

'Is almost set to go. You'll get credit for the designs, of course' *—and the blame when the collection fails—* 'and you'll be free to set yourself up doing whatever you want. Except this time, you won't have to go looking for pearls. This time the whole world will be your oyster.'

She hesitated, and he could see he almost had her, just as he'd always known he would. *Because he knew her type only too well.*

He pressed home his advantage. 'The chance of a fresh start,' he argued softly. 'With as much money as you'll ever need.'

Suddenly—*unexpectedly*—she shook her head. 'No,' she insisted. 'There's no way I could do that. You're forgetting

Laurence. He wanted me to stay and help manage the company. He didn't want me to take the money and run. He knew the business would need some kind of continuity.'

Zane threw his hands up in the air, as much with frustration at her sudden turn-around as with the slight to his management skills. He might have been away from the business for a few years, but who the hell was *she* to doubt his talents? 'I grew up in this business! I led the most aggressive and successful merchant-banking operation in London. And you think I'm not capable of taking over from my father?'

She surveyed him coolly after his outburst. 'Your father clearly had doubts.'

He clamped his mouth shut over a hissed breath. Oh, for someone who looked like a goddess, her words came with an acid burn. If she was trying to drive his price up, she was doing a damned fine job of it. Yet no price would be too large to have her gone!

'I'll pay you out,' he reiterated, the words squeezed out between his teeth. 'I'll pay a premium of twenty per cent on the shares' worth. You'll walk away with a fortune. You won't get a better deal anywhere.'

Her eyes widened. 'You'd pay me that much?'

More, he knew, if that's what it took. 'Then you'll take it?'

She shook her head and again his hopes dived.

'Keep your precious money, Zane. I'm not in the market for a better deal. Because you've just confirmed what I'd already suspected. I can't sell my shares and leave you to take over completely. Do you really think I could abandon the employees' ten per cent share to your mercy? What chance would they have? You'd probably do your best to steamroller them just as you're trying to steamroller me.'

'I'll take care of them.'

'I don't think so. Because if your management skills mirror

your people skills, then this company is in major trouble. There's no way I'd leave you to run this company on your own.'

He swallowed his pride and asked the one question he thought he'd never hear himself ask. 'So, how much do you want?'

It was a victory of sorts. Even she could see that. No matter that he was no doubt still regarding her as some kind of gold-digger, out to extract whatever she could from his father's business while she had the chance. He'd all but pounced on her earlier hesitation as confirmation of his prejudices. And she *had* hesitated, because for a few moments the prospect of leaving had seemed so attractive—the thought of escaping from this incessant sparring, the thought of never seeing Zane again, was like a siren's song calling out to her in her mind. Especially when the alternative, staying in Broome, was the last thing she wanted to do. She didn't want to work alongside Zane. That future was fraught with turmoil and danger and constant conflict, *but be damned if she'd let him drive her out*.

'You don't get it,' she told him. 'I don't want your money. You can't buy me out of this company.'

'*Everyone* has a price.'

She looked up at him and smiled. 'Then maybe you should just face the fact you can't afford mine!'

'You won't stay,' he warned. 'You won't last ten minutes after I return from London, if you're here that long. And then you'll beg for me to buy you out. Then you'll take the money and run!'

She curled one lip up at him. 'There's no way I'll sell out to you. I'd sooner *die* than leave you in charge!

Damn this weather! Zane pushed back in his leather executive chair and locked his arms together high above his head, stretching shoulders and muscles weary from long days and nights at his desk reorganising his business holdings. Outside his office, small hail crashed horizontally into the windows, leaving icy trails down the glass and rendering his prime city view a blurry mess of grey.

It was supposed to be spring, but for the last few days he'd seen enough sleet to last a lifetime. And for the first time in his life he couldn't wait to get back to Broome. Because right now Zane needed sunshine and heat. He needed colour and contrast that only Broome could provide, from the fertile green mangroves to the azure blue waters of Roebuck Bay; from the red pindar dust of the dirt roads leading out of town to the pristine white sands of Cable Beach.

And he needed to see one particular woman....

He jerked upright in his chair and slammed his fists down hard against the desk.

Damn Ruby Clemenger!

From the moment he'd arrived back in London, instead of concentrating on how he would defray the management of his European interests, his mind had been gate-crashed with non-stop visions of Ruby, sending his mind reeling and his plans into disarray. No wonder it had taken him longer to organise his affairs than he'd expected; it had been impossible to concentrate on affairs of business when he had in mind affairs of a much more carnal nature. The visions had plagued him by day, the dreams had tormented him at night and the hunger gnawed at his insides like a vicious rodent seeking escape.

Visions of her lying naked on his bed, her hair splayed across his pillow, framing her face, her eyes wild with need. Dreams of being tangled together with her, satisfying that need in the best way he knew how. But it was the hunger that was the worst of all. Hunger for a woman's honey-gold limbs wrapped around him, holding him to her, her head thrown back in ecstasy while he took them both over the edge...

He must be going mad! Why should his father's mistress

stir such thoughts in his mind? She might be beautiful, she might feel like honeyed perfection in his hands, but she wasn't for him. She never had been.

His father had seen to that!

He growled as he closed down his notebook computer. It had been a long time since he'd had a woman. Too long. And it was no help at all that the woman he thought most about right now was off-limits, even if she hadn't been half a world away.

He made a few quick calls before shrugging into his coat and heading for the elevator. His work here was mostly done—his second-in-charge could handle any residual matters, it was time he was handed responsibility, anyway.

Because he needed to get back to Broome. And it had nothing to do with the visions, nothing to do with the dreams or the hunger. In fact, it made good business sense. Because the sooner he got back to Broome, the sooner he could fix up whatever mess she'd made in his absence.

This late at night the slick city streets were quiet fodder for the Porsche's throaty appetite. He pulled up in front of his terraced house, the caged street trees dancing erratically in the squalls, the reflections from the street lights making crazy patterns on the wet roads, and a welcoming light glowing in his downstairs reception room.

Three weeks to the day! Ruby dragged in a breath, battling to downplay the shivers zipping along her spine as she forced her eyes from the desk calendar. But of course she was nervous! The Passion Collection launch was barely two short months away and there was still so much to do—it had nothing to do with Zane's imminent return.

Her eyes drifted from the piece of jewellery she was examining one final time and back to the calendar. Who was she trying to kid? Twenty-one days he'd been gone and for each one of those days she'd looked at the calendar and wondered, when would he return?

And was he thinking about her as much as she was thinking about him?

Damn the man! She didn't want to think about him—didn't want to have anything to do with him. So why was it that even while he was away she couldn't get him out of her mind? Why was it that, even when she was asleep, her dreams were filled with visions of Zane—troubling, heated images that left her sheets knotted and her body strangely aching come first light?

It was like slow torture, this incessant wondering. He'd skirted around any mention of his return in the infrequent business phone calls they'd had. He'd avoided any mention in their email communication. And so with every passing day her sense of dread grew. But it had to end soon. He wouldn't leave her here for too long to manage on her own. He wouldn't stay in London a day longer than it took.

He'd be back.

Back to claim his inheritance.

Back to make her life hell!

She shuddered, and the heavy piece in her hand slipped through her fingers and on to the desk, breaking her out of her thoughts.

'Think!' she demanded of herself, as she picked up the magnificent pendant, the centrepiece of the Passion Collection, checking it to ensure her clumsiness hadn't harmed the precious piece, and her favourite from the collection.

Slowly she spun the magnificent item in her fingers, its delicate ribbons of yellow gold and *pavé*-set diamonds interspersed with strategically placed gold South Sea pearls. At first glance it could be taken merely as a beautiful piece, a successful juxtaposition of art, science and the best that Mother

Nature could provide. But at a certain angle, in certain lighting, another image emerged. Two lovers intertwined, their skin tones captured in the warm lustre of the pearls, their bodies entwined by golden limbs, their passion for ever captured in the warm glow of one thousand tiny diamonds.

A thrill of achievement coursed through her veins as she cradled the piece in her palm. She'd done it! It was the most wondrous piece she'd ever created, the illusion a triumph.

So why was it that images from her heated dreams invaded her thoughts right now? Why should her body tingle with that now familiar prickle of need?

Why should the pendant remind her of Zane?

For once the burr of the telephone was a welcome intrusion. She listened to her harried PA for a few moments before responding. 'It's okay, Claudette. Put her through.'

She heard a dull click and then, 'I want to speak to Zane, not another secretary!' The cool Nordic accent was no match for the heat of her delivery.

Ruby took a breath, her interest piqued. 'I'm sorry, but at the moment Zane isn't in the office. I'm Ruby Clemenger, can I help?'

'Oh.' There was a pause at the other end. 'You're Ruby? Zane's told me all about you,' she added, her voice changing tone, softer and less aggressive and so much more sexy that it almost purred with satisfaction. 'Zane tells me you're quite beautiful.'

Ruby was rendered speechless. Zane had been talking about her to this woman? *And he'd said that?* Rallying her fractured thoughts, she managed, 'And you are?'

'Anneleise Christiansen.' There was a pause, and then, 'Surely Zane's told you about me?'

Not even once, thought Ruby, curiosity warring with suspicion—clearly this woman was no mere business associate!

But then they'd never really had time to discuss anything, not when they were always sparring with each other over the business. There'd never been a chance to get beyond Laurence and the Bastiani Corporation. 'Of course he has, Anneleise,' she lied, giving the expected response. 'But I'm sorry, I'm not sure when he'll be back. Did you want to leave a message?'

'Oh…I just wanted to make sure he made it back to Broome safely—it's such a very long journey and he looked so tired when he kissed me goodbye.'

He'd kissed her goodbye? Oh, no, Anneleise was definitely no business associate. The candid reality of the situation washed over her like a cold wave. She scrambled to focus on the caller, attempting to think logically, but still it didn't stop the images invading her mind—images of Zane kissing someone else, *wanting* someone else, having to tear himself away from the woman with the sex-kitten voice to return to Broome, tired from too much kissing, *too much sex*.

Not that it should matter. She didn't care who he slept with, it wasn't as if Zane really meant anything to her—she didn't even like the man!

So why then had she spent so much of the last three weeks thinking about him? What the hell was wrong with her?

She'd *known* what a bastard Zane was from the very beginning, abandoning his father for so many years without a word, talking about him as if he'd somehow ruined Zane's life! She'd known *exactly* what kind of man he was, and yet still she'd dreamt of him at night, thinking forbidden thoughts, feeling secret things, waking up wanting and strangely unquenched.

How could she have let herself fall victim to his power, if only in her dreams, when he'd only ever treated her like some gold-digging mistress from the start?

She'd been crazy to let her mind be used that way. But now

that she knew he had the no doubt lovely Anneleise back in London waiting for him—never again!

'He'll be sorry he missed you,' she offered at last, thrusting her wayward thoughts aside. 'I'll let him know you rang when he gets in.'

'Oh, and in case he comes in too late to call here, please tell him…' The voice at the end of the line faltered and paused. Ruby heard what sounded suspiciously like a sob. 'I'm doing my best, like he said—trying not to think about just how far away he is.'

Ruby put the phone down, a tumble of emotions and thoughts assailing her. She wasn't disappointed he had a girlfriend, she wouldn't let herself be. That kind of man was bound to have a dozen girlfriends or mistresses or both. So that cold wash of sensation she'd felt when she'd realised who Anneleise was must have had more to do with relief than anything.

In fact, she ought to be grateful to Anneleise for calling. All the times Zane had seemed so physically threatening, all the times he'd invaded her space and consumed her oxygen, the time he'd handled the pendant at her throat—the touch of his fingertips like a scorching brand; the time he'd run the back of his hand down her body, so softly and yet with such devastating effect—he'd done all of those things merely to unsettle her, to make her uneasy and uncomfortable and afraid. They were part of his inventory of tactics, designed to improve his chances of making her leave. And hadn't those tactics almost convinced her before!

She wouldn't fall for that again.

At least now when Zane returned she wouldn't embarrass herself edging around him, half anticipating him making a move on her, and overreacting if he did. She could be cool and professional.

She picked up the passion pendant once again, twirling the work of art in her fingers, wondering how she could do some things so well, how she could get others so wrong. The pendant's inner image mocked her. How she'd ever designed it was a mystery to her—what did she know of passion and romance, anyway? Her history proved she was one very sad judge of men.

It was good to be back. Zane closed his eyes and let the streaming water cascade over his head, neck and shoulders, massaging muscles wearied by hours stuck in a plane. But in spite of the long flight he felt extraordinarily alive, as if just walking out of the plane into Broome's tropical air had reinvigorated him.

He snapped off the hot water, giving his body a sudden and very necessary cold burst. The extra few days he'd spent with Anneleise had done little to take the edge off his need.

He dried and dressed quickly, noting the time. It was getting late, but he had no doubt Ruby would still be at the office. Intentionally he'd avoided any word of when he would return. He wanted to surprise her and give her no chance of covering up anything she didn't want him to see. By now she'd no doubt agree she wasn't cut out to run anything, let alone a business as complex as the Bastiani Corporation. By now she might be more than ready to accept his generous offer.

What he hadn't expected was the gut-punch reaction to seeing her again. He found her sitting in the workroom, making notes as she sat at the long central bench, her sun-streaked hair coiled behind her head, the look on her face intense as she concentrated on the items displayed around her. Around her, more work benches lined the walls, the racks of delicate tools neatly stacked, a colourful mural on the end wall making up for the lack of any natural light except from the narrowest of windows set up high in the maximum-security room.

Under the artificial lighting, even surrounded by some of the most precious gems on earth, she was the brightest and most beautiful object here. The crossover dress she was wearing accentuated the generous swell of her breasts and her narrow waist. The stool below hid nothing of the feminine curves of her behind or the long, fine sweep of her legs tucked together underneath. His mouth went dry. No wonder his father had wanted her. No wonder his father had taken her for his own!

His hands clenched into fists as he stood watching her. What was she doing here, anyway, playing with her jewels? Surely there was real work that needed to be done!

'What are you doing?'

She jumped at the sound of his voice, her head snapping around. Her eyes spent but a moment taking him in, clearly surprised at being interrupted, before instantly freezing over. She turned straight back to her work and continued making notes.

'So you're back,' she said dismissively. 'Good trip?'

He registered an uncomfortable rumble of frustration. He'd expected more of a reaction than this bored disinterest. Where was the panic? Where was the rush to cover her tracks? And where was her physical reaction to his return?

'Getting ready for the launch?' he asked, moving from his place near the door, drawn to her in spite of himself, curious after so many weeks to once more breathe in her scent and see if it was just the way he'd remembered.

'Given the launch is only weeks away,' she said without looking up, 'the question might be considered redundant.'

'And, of course, nothing else is happening between now and then with the business.'

She looked up sharply. 'Your point being?'

'As you say, the launch is weeks away. Couldn't what

you're doing wait for a more appropriate time? Aren't there more pressing matters to deal with in the meantime?'

'And you'd be the best judge of what a "more appropriate time" is, I imagine, given you've been away for three weeks.'

'Why are you always so argumentative?'

'You might ask yourself the same question.'

His teeth ground together at her reply. But he was closer now, so close that he had an answer for that first silent question of his. He breathed in her scent, tasting it on his tongue, and he felt a strange, familiar heat move through him. If possible, she smelt even better than he remembered. Fresher. More alive.

More woman.

'I thought you might like to have dinner with me.' He heard himself speak the words and wondered what the hell he was thinking. He'd been planning on coming back, all guns blazing. But now… 'There's a lot that's happened the last few weeks we should catch up on.'

'You think?' she responded absently, studiously ignoring his presence opposite the bench as she reached for a pair of pearl earrings suspended on golden spirals, examining them closely before jotting down a couple more notes.

What the hell was she playing at! Three weeks ago she'd reacted to him like a woman should. She'd been warm and sensual, her body and her femininity responding to him even while her mouth spat fire. And that was just the way he wanted it. Not that he was interested in her for himself, his father had seen to that. He was more interested in the shares his father had bequeathed her, and if he could make her more uncomfortable about staying and holding on to them, then so much the better. So, what had happened in the interim that she could be so cool towards him? Whatever it was, he didn't like it.

'What do you think you're doing?' he demanded.

'The running sheet for the launch. We've got three models flying in from Europe, all with different colouring. I'm working out which model should wear what. Darker hair will suit some designs better than blonde, but they have to co-ordinate with the designer clothes we've arranged for them, as well. It's too important to be left to chance on the night.'

'No!' he insisted. 'Not that.'

'Then what?' she asked innocently enough, but still without returning his gaze.

'Look at me,' he said, sick of talking to the top of her head.

'I'm busy right now, Zane, and it's late. Can this wait until tomorrow?'

'*Look* at me!'

She froze and for a few moments her breathing was her only movement. Then she replaced the earrings, clasped her hands together on the bench and looked up at him, her eyes wide like a schoolgirl brought to task by her teacher.

'Yes?'

Her cool eyes and bland expression fired up his temperature. What was going on? She was no ice-virgin. It was all he could do not to lunge over the bench and take that oh-so-innocent face in his hands and kiss those lips senseless, until she'd shed this ridiculous attitude and was begging him to make love to her.

And he was only too ready to oblige!

She should never have looked up.

Immediately Ruby longed to turn away from those brooding eyes, that demanding expression and the entire domineering package, but she dared not now. She couldn't back down. And she wouldn't have to, not if she remembered what kind of man he was.

He's arrogant, she reminded herself, starting off a checklist of his shortcomings, *he's bitter and resentful at his father's treatment of him, no matter how well deserved*. And, given the fact he'd kept Anneleise a complete secret, not entirely honourable while he'd feigned interest in her. Was he so low as to stoop to two-timing? She couldn't put it past him, not that she'd be giving him the opportunity!

'All right,' she said with new resolve, angling her chin higher in defiance, 'now you have my undivided attention, what's so important?'

'Have you nearly finished what you're doing?'

'Does it matter?'

'The running sheet! Have you nearly finished?'

He stood over her glowering, his hands planted wide on the bench, his body leaning dangerously towards hers. She tried to ignore the width of his shoulders, the power in his muscled arms as they braced tight against the bench. She battled to keep her eyes away from the vee at his open neck, where the olive skin gleamed under its dusting of dark curls.

She swallowed. 'Maybe, for now. But I don't see—'

'Then I'm taking you out.'

She started to shake her head. 'There's no need—'

'It's getting late. You have to eat.' He leaned closer, until he filled her field of vision and his masculine aura filled the air around her, so thick and intense that she could almost taste it. But what was worse—*much worse* for someone who'd decided he wouldn't affect her any more—his presence triggered a hunger inside her that no mere meal would assuage. He was so fresh from his shower that his dark hair still curled damply above his collar, with his scent infused by nothing more than pure unadulterated essence of man. She swallowed. She had to get out of here.

'And,' he pressed, 'we have matters to discuss. I need a full report on this launch of yours,' he continued. 'You're spending one hell of a lot of money shipping in models and celebrity guests.'

'The budget's already been approved—'

'Not by me! I want a full report.'

She pushed herself up straight, fighting off the unwelcome tingling awareness in her flesh that seemed to follow breathing him in. Damn, but how could he still affect her this way after all she knew about him? She must be more tired than she thought. She needed sleep, deep, uninterrupted sleep, for a chance to build her defences, a chance to overcome this annoying vulnerability that accompanied her weariness. So tomorrow they might talk, but tonight she was determined to sleep.

'Can't I deliver you a report tomorrow, Zane?' she suggested, sliding off the stool, needing to put more distance between them. She started collecting up her papers and slotting jewellery back in secure boxes. 'It's getting late and you must be tired after the flight.'

He moved around the bench to her side, short-circuiting her plans for escape. 'Are you pretending that in all the time I was away, nothing happened in a business this size that I should be informed about now?'

'I sent you emails. Didn't you read them?'

'I read what you sent me.'

'Then that's all there is to know.'

'There's nothing more? Nothing else you had any concerns about?'

She looked up at him, resentful of the way his voice dripped with disbelief. So, to add to her sins, now he thought she was incompetent, incapable of looking after the business she'd been helping Laurence with for years.

'Actually, you're right, Zane. Something did happen that I

should have told you about. I'm sorry it didn't occur to me, not that it will take long to fill you in.'

'Well?' he said.

She locked away the last gems, snapped her notes into her portfolio and stood, facing him. 'You had a message from your girlfriend. She was hoping you'd made it back okay seeing how tired you looked when you kissed her goodbye.'

CHAPTER SIX

HE HESITATED BARELY a second. 'Anneleise called here?'

His words shouldn't have made a dent on her victorious exit. It had felt so good taking this man by surprise that she'd been almost gleeful as she'd made her way out of the room. And yet those very same words—'*Anneleise called here?*'—confirmed what she'd suspected, that Zane had a woman waiting for him back in London, and suddenly she knew there'd been no mistake, no misunderstanding. His interest in her had nothing to do with attraction and everything to do with intimidation.

And somehow her victory didn't feel quite so satisfying any more. Somehow it felt flat and empty, and it shouldn't have, because that would mean she cared, and she didn't, not really, and that only made her angrier.

She spun around, sick of the deception, sick of the lies and the pressure-cooker situation she found herself in every time she met up with this man. 'Of course it was Anneleise!' she snapped. 'I don't believe you, Zane. Exactly how many girl-friends do you have?'

'Anneleise is hardly my girlfriend.'

She blinked her surprise, realising he'd moved closer while her back was turned, so much closer that his nearness took her unawares and made her take a step backwards against the bench.

'Your mistress, then.'

'And that would bother you, would it, that I have a mistress?'

'Not at all,' she insisted, looking anywhere but at him. 'Your private life is no concern of mine.'

He said nothing, but when her eyes found him again it was to witness the corners of his mouth slowly turn up. Somewhere his eyes had found a glint that gave them an edge—heat, power, *danger*—setting off a sudden bloom of warm tingles inside. Her breath caught as she battled uselessly to quell the reaction.

'Forget Anneleise,' he said, moving closer. 'She's just an old friend. You don't need to feel jealous of her.'

'Oh, no,' she protested, shaking her head. She wasn't jealous! She didn't care! 'You've got the wrong idea.'

He smiled a wolfish smile of disbelief that made much too rapid a change to another expression—more intent—more urgent.

More ravenous.

'I missed you,' he admitted, his voice low and rough. 'I missed your arguments and your flashing blue eyes and most of all I missed how good it felt to touch you.' He lifted one hand and smoothed a loose tendril of hair behind her ear. She shuddered as his fingers grazed her ear, mesmerised by his words, her pulse hammering so loud in her veins she was sure he would feel its frantic beat.

His head tilted closer, his eyes forcing hers to lock with his and his fingers cupping her chin. 'Did you think about me while I was gone?'

'I…' She blinked, casting her eyes from side to side, working out the quickest route to escape. 'I honestly don't recall. I had a lot to think about.'

This time he laughed, throaty and low in a way that warmed her spine to melting point and made her forget all about running. 'That's a shame, because I did. I thought about you a lot. You cost me a lot of sleep.'

'That's a pity,' she said with a lot more bravado than she felt. 'Maybe you can take something for it.'

'Oh,' he said, his lips just a whisper from her own, his eyes seductive, their holding power like a magnet. 'I intend to….'

Time slowed between them, her world suddenly shrunken to that split-second of understanding, to that hitched breath of anticipation that came in the moments before a kiss. Already she could feel his lips on hers. Already she could taste him. Already she was welcoming him….

Momentarily he noticed her aqua eyes change, swirling with questions and uncertainty, but then his focus moved wholly to the sensation of meeting her lips. He welcomed their tentative warmth, he revelled in their sweetness. With his free arm he circled her waist to prevent any sudden retreat, as the hand cupping her chin swept around her neck, but aside from one initial bolt of shock she made no attempt to escape. Emboldened, he moved deeper into the kiss. She was warm and lush and the way she tasted in his mouth, the way her curves fitted so tantalisingly against his body, only ramped up his desire.

His lips moved over hers, softly, caressing, *coaxing*. Damn, but she was sweet. He'd known she'd taste good, but he'd had no idea just how much. He'd known she felt good, but he'd had no idea how much better she'd feel pressed up close against him.

Her hands appeared at his waist, her fingers settling and curling into his shirt as if unsure, hesitant. He trawled in a breath at the contact. It was a start—she was touching him, and he willed her to explore further. It wasn't enough to feel her hands through his shirt, he wanted to feel her hands tight against his skin, her nails biting into his flesh. He wanted to feel her naked body glide under his.

He wanted her. Now!

He found the slide clamping her hair. A squeeze of the ends reaped immediate benefits as the length spilled free, tumbling down over her shoulders. He let the clasp fall unheeded to the bench behind as he spread his fingers wide through the unravelling coils of her hair, enjoying the play of the silken strands over his hand and directing her head exactly where his mouth wanted her.

He shifted her away from the bench, enjoying the curve of her behind under his hand, using it to press her hungrily into contact with his aching need as he left her lips to trail hot kisses down the line of her throat. A second hand joined the first, lifting her, pulling her against him and higher...

What the hell was she thinking? The clatter of her hair clip broke through the sensual fog he'd spun around her. Her eyes flew open to the harsh light of reality while even now the liquid warmth of his kisses urged her to close her eyes and give herself up to sensation again.

But that was exactly her problem—she hadn't been thinking at all. And look where it had got her—plastered against him, the bold evidence of his arousal between them, shocking yet sensual, firing up her body and turning her mind completely away from logic to matters much more primitive.

The hands now knotted in his shirt fisted in the fabric and pushed, trying to make distance between them even as his lips ascended the line of her throat to her mouth again. She swallowed and turned her head away, her hands pressing hopelessly against his firm torso. So much strength, so much muscled power lay beneath her hands, so much to resist. And her body felt so weak, so languid and liquid, her spine soft and yielding, her breasts hyper-sensitive and welcoming of every tiny graze against his shirt. But she had to resist!

His mouth sought hers, his hand steering her head closer.

'Zane,' she urged, turning her head, resisting the pressure. 'Stop this.'

His mouth worked the line of her jaw while one hand slid up around between them, cupping one breast almost reverentially, squeezing it so tenderly she almost reeled from the simple and yet utterly sensual wave of pleasure that roiled through her.

'You want this,' he whispered huskily against her skin so that even his words were a caress. 'I can feel it.' Then he brushed his thumb over her peaked nipple and she shuddered anew as a battery of sensations assailed her, setting her core ablaze and melting her closer to him, when being closer was the last thing she needed.

In desperation she summoned the most potent weapon she had in her defence.

'And what do you want?' she demanded in a quavering voice she barely recognised as her own. 'To find out how you rate compared to your father?'

He let her go as if she were poison, thrusting her away from him without a word. Shakily, she seemed to come to terms with her sudden release and made her swift withdrawal from his presence, one eye over her shoulder watching him guardedly, waiting for him in case he struck again. But he didn't move. He let her go and only when she had removed herself from the offices completely did he let his fist slam hard into the surface of the bench.

The crunch of bone and flesh against the solid bench top hardly registered. But then, nothing could feel worse than the self-disgust he felt for himself right now. Three weeks had turned him into nothing more than an animal! He would have had her—he could have had her—right here tonight. He was so close to lifting her atop the bench and pushing himself between her thighs and taking her….

He would have taken his father's mistress!

So much for believing himself a notch up on the evolutionary scale. He was no better than his father. No better than the man he held in such low esteem. He made his way out to his car, absently rubbing his fist in his other hand, still burning with need, high on testosterone.

High on self-loathing.

It was bad enough that Ruby had slept with his father. It was bad enough that she'd loved him and had been his mistress.

But his real problem was why, in spite of all that, he still wanted her.

She should never have let him kiss her! How could she pretend that she didn't want his advances, how could she claim she was unaffected by his sheer magnetism when she had all but given him an open invitation?

For two days they'd avoided each other, managing for the most part to stay out of each other's way, barely speaking beyond a grunt when they came across each other, but that wouldn't last, Ruby knew, as she switched on her desktop computer and put her purse in her desk. They couldn't run the company that way. Sooner or later they were going to have to talk. She looked down at her diary notes and swallowed when she saw what her PA had registered alongside nine-thirty.

Meeting with Zane—boardroom.

She knew there were matters to discuss—Zane was still waiting for her report on the launch budget and there was a visit to the opening of the imminent pearl harvest to organise—but knowing there was work to be done wasn't enough to stop the overwhelming sense of dread surrounding her. She didn't want to see Zane; she didn't want to be exposed to him or his powerful magnetism. *Didn't want to be attracted to him!*

"You want this," he'd told her, and he'd been right, and no amount of denying it would make a difference. She'd let him kiss her—it had been her choice. She'd allowed him to caress her, to touch her intimately like he possessed her and she'd enjoyed it and she'd wanted more. She'd wanted to be swept away.

She'd wanted to be possessed.

And she could have been, if she hadn't snapped to her senses. But even then, it hadn't been her determination that had saved her. It had been Laurence. Just as he'd protected her once before when she'd needed help, so he was her shield now.

Just how long would Zane believe they'd been lovers? And what would happen if he discovered the truth? What good would she be to Bastiani Corporation then—unable to leave if she was to carry out Laurence's wishes, unable to live with herself if she succumbed to what her body craved?

It must never happen.

He was waiting for her when she got there, firmly entrenched at the head of the table, his face grim, the tapping pencil in his hand signalling his impatience, although the clock on the wall behind clearly showed she was barely a minute late.

'Nice of you to join me at last,' he snapped.

She smiled as sweetly as she could under the circumstances. 'Oh, I assure you, the pleasure is all mine.'

She could see his jaw grinding in response, his lips itching to let go with another sarcastic jibe and she knew he was still angry with himself for what had almost happened two nights before. And that suited her just fine. The angrier he was, the easier it was to forget how he'd made her feel and the easier it would be to repel him.

He waited while she sat down two places from him,

twisting the pencil between his fingers. No way was she going to sit any closer to his humming tension.

'Right,' he said, 'let's start with that report you promised me on the launch budget.'

Two hours later Ruby felt like she'd been tumble-dried, her mind reeling from the relentless interrogation she'd just been subjected to, but if he was impressed by the way she'd defended and fought for and justified every last dollar to be spent, he didn't show it. Instead, his mood seemed to be getting blacker by the minute.

They ran through the remaining items on the agenda more quickly, working out security arrangements for the launch, sparring over a small change to employee conditions Ruby had proposed and making plans for a visit the next week to one of the pearl farms for the start of the upcoming harvest. Ruby wasn't keen on accompanying Zane, but the pearl-farming business had changed a lot since he was last involved and it was important that she passed on things that she'd learned, now that Laurence wasn't around to teach Zane himself.

That matter finally settled, Ruby started collecting her papers to leave, when he spoke.

'One last thing,' Zane began. 'I think it's time we set down some ground rules for how the business should be managed. Here's how I see things working. Now that I'm back in Broome, I'll take over the day-to-day management of the company and you can go back to design work full time.'

Ruby felt her blood pressure surge as she sank back into her chair. She dredged up a thin smile. 'I appreciate that you're so interested in my input in making these ground rules and in ensuring I have time for my design work, but I actually enjoy the managerial side of the business, Zane, so I'd prefer to keep my hand in if it's all the same to you.'

One glance at his scowling face was more than enough to tell her that it wasn't the same to him.

'That will hardly be necessary,' he countered. 'I'm in charge now. And you'll have a chance to focus on what you're employed here to do.'

'You seem to forget I'm not just "employed" here now. I actually own almost half of the business, a business I was helping to manage in addition to my design work before Laurence died.'

'My father was sick. I won't need your help.'

'Laurence wasn't always sick. *Plus*, I believe my share in the company entitles me to a say in how the business is managed—just as your father obviously intended.'

His nostrils flared and a vein in his temple pulsed dangerously in the silence that followed her comment.

'Don't make the mistake,' he warned softly, the dark storm cells of his eyes never leaving hers, 'of making this more difficult than it has to be.'

His quiet words carried like a threat in the super-charged atmosphere and she only hoped her blue eyes relayed the ice-cold hostility she felt for him right now.

'Or what?' she challenged. 'You'll kiss me again?'

The pencil between Zane's fingers snapped. She held her breath as the pieces tumbled from his fingers and clattered on to the table, a sound that only served to ramp up the tense atmosphere.

Zane didn't care about the pencil. His head was pounding and his eyes were too busy burning up a trail from her eyes to her sweet lips. Oh, yeah, they sure were sweet. Lush and tangy like ripe tropical fruit and only too eager to open under his and be devoured, despite her protestations. And now she was daring him to kiss her?

Not a chance!

He shifted his gaze back to her eyes again and allowed himself a smile, feeling for the first time today that he had the upper hand at last.

'If that's what you're hoping for, then I'm afraid you're in for a big disappointment.'

He left the room before she could protest, satisfied he'd got in the last word and smug in the knowledge that he'd survived the entire meeting, resisting the urge to throw her on to the boardroom table and finish the job he'd started two nights before.

He could resist her, despite her lush curves and her sweet mouth.

He would resist her. And, dammit, he'd show her her rightful place in the process!

CHAPTER SEVEN

TWO HOURS NORTH of Broome, in a pristine and sheltered cove off the Kimberley coast of red cliffs and green mangroves and pure white sand, the boat met up with the operations vessel that would manage the harvest of the first of Bastiani's ten pearl farms. Here the waters were clear and blue, the oysters lying below the surface of the water in panels attached to long lines in order for them to sway back and forth with the flow of the rich tides.

Ruby lifted her face to the sky and breathed in the warm salt-tinged air as the high-speed launch nudged alongside the operations vessel. It was so good to be away from the tension-laden air of the office, not that the source of that tension had remained there.

Today he looked more relaxed than she'd ever seen him, in tailored shorts and polo top, his thick dark hair whipping around his face as the power boat had made its exhilarating trip along the coast, his sunglasses hiding eyes she'd sensed were parked long and intense on her if the prickling sensation in her skin was any indication.

Their meeting a few days ago had precipitated a frosty intolerance between them in the office. Whenever possible, they'd avoided each other. When it was unavoidable that they had to meet, they'd grated on each other like icebergs passing through the same narrow strait. But underneath the chill, Ruby had felt his heat, the seething resentment leaching from him like a life-force, his eyes always tracking her movements like a predator. Watching. Waiting.

Why did he persist? If he'd accepted she was off-limits, why did he still watch her? Why couldn't he just leave her be? Or was he merely determined to get rid of her any way he could and he'd decided that making her uncomfortable, bombarding her constantly with this knife-edge tension, was the way to do it?

Damn him, he wouldn't be rid of her that easily!

She gathered up her few things as the boats bumped together over the light swell, determined not to let him undermine her trip today. There was a real buzz of excitement among everyone to be here at the start of a new harvest and Ruby felt an enormous sense of expectancy. Every pearl was special, but there were some that caught a designer's eye, some that simply begged to be set off in the perfect setting. Right now she couldn't wait to see what new opportunities the harvest turned up.

She turned to the side of the boat to find Zane offering his hand to assist her as she climbed from the fast launch up on to the operations vessel. His eyes were masked by dark glasses, his jaw tight and for a moment she drew back. The last time they'd touched each other… But he was only offering a hand and it would be churlish to refuse, so with a hesitant nod she held out her hand, allowing him to wrap it securely with his larger one, anchoring her to him as she clambered up and over. She jumped to the deck alongside, wanting their contact to be as brief as possible. But he used his leverage to pull her closer before she landed, so that she had to reach out a hand to his chest to stop herself from falling into him.

She looked up into his face, suddenly breathless, her heart racing irrationally and with the innate knowledge that under those dark glasses his eyes burned hot and heavy.

'Thank you,' she managed to say, *I think*, as she stepped back, peeling her hand from his chest before her fingers had the chance to curl and test the firm, muscled flesh just millimetres below.

The grim set of his mouth curled just enough to hint at a smile before it disappeared behind a sigh. He sucked in a breath and released her, turning away instead to greet the operations vessel manager.

Ruby blinked and gathered her thoughts as the manager welcomed them aboard before giving them a brief tour of the vessel, introducing them to the crew as they went. Then they waited while the first panels of oysters were recovered from the sea and watched, fascinated, as the shells were prised open just enough to remove the treasure within.

In awe, they watched silently as the technician used a pair of long tweezers to remove a perfect pearl from the very first oyster before skilfully seeding the shell with another bead, slightly larger this time, and then releasing the clamp from the shell and completing the operation.

Several times they watched this process, marvelling at the treasure revealed after the shells had been submerged for years beneath the sea.

'How long since you've seen this process?' Ruby whispered to him as the technicians continued their delicate work.

'Too long to remember,' he admitted honestly, totally fascinated by a world that should be all too familiar to him, but which suddenly seemed new and exciting. 'Things have come a long way. I remember they used to bring the shell to shore to perform these operations.'

She nodded, as the technician repeated the process on the

shells from the next panel, discarding the few that hadn't lived up to expectations for shell and pearl meat. 'This way ensures the oysters are disturbed for the shortest time possible. The yields have increased considerably.'

It made good business sense, and not for the first time Zane was bitterly reminded of what he'd missed out on over the last few years. While he'd been carving his own career out in Europe, trying to prove his point, his father had still been innovating, still improving the business. And for many of the years he'd been away, Ruby had been by his father's side.

And she'd learned something in that time, from what he'd seen—certainly more than what he'd first given her credit for. He shifted slightly, not entirely comfortable with the knowledge that there was more to Ruby than a pleasingly arranged set of physical attributes. Mind you, out here, where they were surrounded by a crew of twenty or more, was the perfect place to appreciate them. He could look, he could admire. Where was the harm in that? He could even touch, like he'd done, taking her hand in his as she'd transferred from the launch and pulling her into him. Out here he could risk that—the touch of her skin, the sweet swell of her curves—without the danger of getting carried away. *Like a taste of forbidden fruit.*

He leaned closer to her now, not because he particularly wanted to ask her another question, but because it was an excuse to get nearer and put his mouth close to her ear and once more breathe in her own individual scent.

'How many pearls will they do today?'

She turned slightly to answer and he caught her aqua eyes flicker with confusion. 'We talked about that on the way out. The vessel should manage around five thousand per day. It should take around ten days to get through the harvest at this particular farm.'

They'd talked about it before? That was news to him. But

then, maybe he'd been more focused on the way she looked, in slim-fitting khaki shorts and a cool white shirt over a white crop top. Not that there was anything overtly sexy about it. Maybe it was the combination of the hip-fitting shorts, the honey-skinned legs, and the mere hint of an outline of a light bra under that fine shirt that did it. Perhaps it was the inch of skin that peeked out so invitingly between her shorts and her knotted shirt whenever she moved the right way. Or maybe it was just that it was her, wrapped up inside it all. Whatever it was, he hadn't been tempted to take his eyes from her the entire trip.

And now she was close enough for him to breathe her in, and to deconstruct all the individual scents that made her up: the tropical tang of her shampoo, the kiss of her subtle body wash, a hint of a perfume, soft and light, and the unmistakable essence of her, heightened by her excitement. It curled into his senses and drew him like a magnet, even when he knew it shouldn't.

Reluctantly he turned his attentions back to the operations and both of them watched intently as the process continued, noting the huge differences in the pearls that were retrieved, each pearl an exciting discovery, some perfectly round, some marked by the constrictions of bands of muscles that had grown about them, some imperfectly shaped and some small ones, called keshi pearls, formed unexpectedly, completely by nature. And the colours were something else. The range went from silver-white to pink and gold and every shade in between, their rich nacre a feature of the South Sea pearl that made them so sought after.

He shared the thrill as each new pearl was discovered. He felt the disappointment when the seeding had failed and he realised how much he'd missed this business. Somehow the cut and thrust of corporate takeover life seemed to pale next to this wild and vivid business.

He looked back at Ruby's profile, her lips plump and slightly parted as she watched the harvest in wonder and awe. And she was so much a part of this business, vital and alive and so fresh.

Forbidden fruit, indeed.

And, oh, so damned tempting.

'The pearls will be graded once they're back in Broome,' Ruby told him as the launch powered its way back. 'We'll keep the best of the gems for future collections and the rest will be exported to other markets overseas.'

He nodded. 'It's good I came out today. So much has changed, even in the space of a decade. It seems my father really knew what he was doing.'

She placed a hand on his forearm and smiled widely up at him like he'd finally said something right. 'Thank you,' she said, her eyes reflecting the aqua of the ocean, the loose tendrils of her hair whipping around her face like they'd come alive.

And her smile reached down deep inside him till it gripped tight and damned near pulled him inside out. He'd never seen her smile like that before and certainly never aimed at him. Completely unexpected it was very, very sexy.

He had to fight the sudden urge to pull her face to his mouth and kiss her senseless. He wanted to feel the way those lips curved under his mouth. He wanted to taste that smile.

And then he'd taste every part of her!

'Thank you for what?' he asked, his voice half-choked, because then he'd already forgotten what she was talking about. Instead he was thinking about that night in the workroom when he'd succumbed to temptation and kissed her, her body supple and pliant and her roundness perfectly filling his hands, cradling his heat. He'd been disgusted with himself for weakening and letting that kiss go so far.

But since then there'd been times he'd regretted he hadn't gone further....

'Thank you,' she answered, 'for finally giving your father credit for something.'

He closed his eyes against the sun, shaking his head as his vision ran blood red. Damn whatever it was she was doing to him!

He didn't want to think about his father right now, and what he thought of him and why, not with her hand resting on his arm and the tendrils of her hair forming a sunkissed halo around her face while thoughts of her he had no right having made him hard.

But if he didn't think about his father, he would likely give in to this inexplicable need he felt for her.

His gut twisted into a knot, hungry and aching for something he couldn't have.

Someone he couldn't have!

He let her hand slip away as he raked his fingers through his hair. For she would never be his. He could never take up where his father had left off. How could he sleep with his father's mistress? How could he make love to the woman his father had bedded? But then, how then could he stay in Broome, living with this insane desire, feeling the need consume him every time she was near, burning to possess her and yet knowing that he never could?

He couldn't live that way! So there was only one answer. *He would have to get rid of her, whatever it took.*

Still locked in his own private machinations, Zane steered the car towards Ruby's hotel. If it wasn't bad enough that he'd been foolish to insist that he drive her to and from the boat dock today, he'd arrived back on land to find a message from Anneleise waiting for him, despite him telling her not to contact him here. So much for sorting things out in London. He would have to do something about her, too. It was also bad enough that she'd turned up at his house uninvited and with a copied key, without pursuing him out here.

Lost in thought, he barely registered it would be night soon, the sun dipping lower, sucking the blue from the sky and transforming it with a pale lemon wash. The colour of the sky was the last thing on his mind. First of all he had to deal with Ruby. He'd go and see the lawyer first chance he had. Derek Finlayson would just have to be made to understand that this arrangement wasn't working, no matter what he believed Laurence had wanted. They couldn't run the company to-gether—not with the way things were between them—not with her history. And if Zane increased his offer for her shares, maybe he could get Finlayson to speak to Ruby and convince her to take it. Maybe she would listen to the lawyer.

Alongside him, Ruby shivered and rubbed her arms.

'Cold?' Zane moved automatically to adjust the air condi-tioning. It was the first they'd spoken since getting into the car. After a few weeks in London the late afternoon air felt warm to him, but he knew that was different for locals. Once acclimatised to the intense, tropical wet season, anything else felt cool by comparison.

'Not really,' she said, rubbing the bridge of her nose. 'I guess I just didn't realise how tired I am. Today was a good change. It's nice to get out of the office.'

An unwelcome twinge of guilt niggled at him. He'd left her to manage the company by herself while he'd taken care of his business back in London with barely a thought to her pro-fessional needs. In fact, he'd been waiting for her to fail, *willing her to fail*. She'd had to handle all her normal design work plus the business side of things that Laurence had be-queathed them both. But in spite of everything he'd believed, she hadn't failed. On the contrary, her business emails during his absence had been to the point, their content clear, and he'd had no need to intervene, no need to question anything she'd recommended, the disasters he'd anticipated never arising.

And then he'd returned and things had got a whole lot more complicated.

He snatched another look sideways while waiting to turn off the highway. The stress had obviously cost her. She'd relaxed back into her chair, her eyes closed, and, highlighted in the sun's setting rays, he could see the shadows under her eyes and the tension that lined her jaw. And yet there was still something about her, the shape of her eyes, the line of her cheek, the fullness of her mouth, generous and inviting. And then there was her body...

She opened her eyes and caught him watching her. Hers widened momentarily, but still she didn't look away. Instead her head tilted slightly and she asked, 'Why do you hate your father so much?'

He turned his attention back to the road, making his turn when it was clear. 'Who says I hate him?'

'Only just about everything you say or do. And the fact you left and didn't bother to contact him for nine years. Today was the first time I've ever heard you say a decent thing about him, but when I mentioned it you clammed up, like you'd broken some vow to yourself never to say a kind word about him.'

That wasn't the reason he'd closed the conversation down, but he was hardly going to tell her what he'd really been thinking about. 'I just call it like I see it.'

'What happened all those years ago that you could just take off like you did? What went wrong?'

Everything, he thought, his knuckles turning white on the steering wheel. *I couldn't bear the sight of him.* 'I had my reasons.'

She was quiet for a moment. Then, 'Does it have anything to do with your mother's death?'

His head snapped around. 'What makes you ask that?' he asked gruffly.

'I don't know. It's just you must have left shortly after she died.'

'She didn't die. She was killed.'

The words hung heavy and full-bodied in the air between them. It didn't make sense. 'Laurence mentioned a car crash.'

'And did he tell you who was driving?'

Desperately she tried to recall the story Laurence had shared with her late one evening after a minor attack some years ago, when he was feeling unusually mortal. 'I'm not sure. But I know it wasn't Laurence, if that's what you're suggesting.'

He laughed, short and bitter as he pulled into the car park opposite the hotel looking over Cable Beach, out to where the sun was a blazing orange-rimmed disc dipping lower and lower towards the ocean in a sky that now glowed in a thousand different shades of gold.

'You're so quick to defend my father! No, he wasn't driving. But did he tell you anything about the woman who was driving the car, the woman who hit the embankment that caused the car to roll over, crushing them both and killing my mother?'

She searched her memory, but whatever he was looking for she couldn't find. 'I don't know. You tell me.'

He exhaled on a long breath, his palms damp and his chest tight like it was bound by steel bands. 'Bonnie Carter,' he squeezed out of lungs bereft of air. 'My mother's best friend since school, her bridesmaid on her wedding day and my godmother. She was just about part of the family.'

'I don't see the significance,' Ruby admitted, her head shaking.

'No? Neither did I until the crash,' he went on, his voice as flat and bereft of life as she'd ever heard. 'Then it all made sense.

'Bonnie was so beautiful. Oh, I always thought my mother was, too, but in a different way. My mother was average height and build, but with a smile that made anything else irrelevant. Whereas Bonnie could have been a model, tall and long legged and with a face that turned heads.' He looked pointedly at her. 'A lot like you. It never occurred to me to wonder back then why she hadn't married.' He swivelled his whole body around towards her, his eyes boring into her with such intensity, with such raw pain, that she flinched from the connection.

'And for all of those years she was playing up to my mother, the perfect best friend, the adoring and generous god-mother—for all of that time she was operating behind my mother's back, secretly servicing my father's needs, being paid to act as my father's whore!'

He thrust open his car door and stepped outside, suddenly needing more space and air around him than was provided by the confines of the car. He walked across the strip of lawn to the wooden railing that marked the edge of the dunes leading down to the beach and sucked in great lungfuls of the fresh Indian Ocean air, trying to fill the vacuum left inside him, trying to vanquish the stale memories of the past.

At that very moment the molten sun dipped silently on the horizon, touching the surface of the ocean, flaring briefly as it merged with the sea. Behind him he heard the muted click of the car's passenger door closing.

He didn't turn. He just gazed over the sea and watched as the ocean accepted the burning sun bit by bit into its depths until its light was just a last desperate pinprick and then nothing. Just as his father had extinguished so completely any prospect of a father-son relationship for them.

'Zane,' he heard Ruby say. 'I'm sorry.'

'It's not your fault,' he replied.

She ignored the bite in his words. 'I just can't believe it, though. Laurence would never have done that to your mother. He was a man of honour, of integrity. He loved Maree. I know he did. You must remember that.'

'Then why did he sleep with Bonnie?' He spun away from the sea and the sunset to face her. 'I'd grown up listening to him advocating integrity and ethics and that family comes first for as long as I could remember, but when it came down to it, he was just a man. A weak man, as it turned out. Laurence admitted as much.'

'But… When?'

'After the crash. My father went crazy, consumed by grief. I discovered he was organising a double funeral and that he was planning to bury both of them in the family plot—together! I knew both women were close, but this was crazy. When I challenged him about it he even had the gall to tell me Bonnie had given him something my mother never could.'

'I can't believe he would betray your mother like that.'

Even in the darkening sky his eyes burned with coal-black fury, dark and resentful. 'Why? Did you think you were the only one who took my father's eye! Did you think you were special?'

He turned back to the sea, one hand wringing his neck, the other hanging loosely by his side. 'When I begged him to deny he'd ever slept with Bonnie, he wouldn't. He couldn't! Because he'd kept Bonnie as his paid mistress and he'd betrayed my mother, and so I walked out of Broome the minute my mother was in the ground. And he never once tried to stop me.'

Quite the contrary. He could still hear his father's heated words ringing in his ears—'You'll never make it on your own'; 'You'll come back crawling on your hands and knees.' But he hadn't come crawling back. And he'd well and truly shown his old man that he could make it on his own.

So why did he feel so hollow?

Surely victory should taste sweeter?

But he'd arrived home too late to make his peace with his father. Too late to hear him admit he was wrong. And too late to stop his father from taking another mistress, this time one he wanted for himself!

Around them the night sky descended, shades of purple deepening to ink black.

Ruby hugged her arms to her chest. It couldn't be true. The Laurence she knew wasn't like that. And yet something must have happened. A chill descended her spine. Could that be the key to Laurence's final words to his son? 'Perhaps,' she started, thinking aloud, 'perhaps that's why—'

She broke off, but he rounded on her. 'That's why *what*?'

She blinked up uncertainly at him and hesitated. She'd never told him. The timing had never been right. It had never made any sense. But maybe now…

She swallowed. 'Maybe that's why your father wanted to apologise.'

'What are you talking about?' he demanded, taking a step closer to her. 'When was this?'

'Just before he died. I was holding his hand and he said, "Tell Zane I'm sorry."'

'His parting words,' he accused, 'intended for *me*, and you didn't think to pass them on!'

'I'm so sorry,' she whispered.

'And that's all he said. *Nothing* more?'

She looked away, out to sea, out to anywhere she wouldn't have to meet those eyes, their glare accusatory, their pain hauntingly vivid. But she wouldn't tell him the rest. '*Look after Zane.*' He didn't have to hear that. He wouldn't want to hear it.

'There was no time for more. The machines started beeping and people came from everywhere. It was the last thing he said. Not that it seemed to make any sense.' She looked back at him, her tone shifting to accusatory. 'You were the one who'd left Broome. You were the one who'd walked away from your own father. Why should he have to apologise to you?'

His breath was fast and furious, his chest pumping air.

'So you chose not to tell me.'

'It wasn't like that!'

'Then tell me, what was it like?'

She opened her mouth to defend herself, wanting to tell him that he'd hated her on sight and no more so than when he'd learned his father had left her half of his inheritance; wanting to protest that somehow they'd never really had the opportunity for a heart-to-heart chat; wanting to shout that it was payback for thinking she had been Laurence's mistress. But she knew in her heart that there was no defence for what she'd done. She'd decided he wasn't worthy of Laurence's apology and she'd made no attempt to tell him. She'd kept words meant for Zane to herself because she didn't understand what they could mean and she'd let Laurence down in the process.

'I'm sorry, Zane,' she said instead. 'I should have told you.'

'I'm speaking to the lawyer first chance I get.' He forced the words through gritted teeth. 'I'll work out a settlement, but I want you out of the business and gone from Broome.'

'But the launch—'

'It's your precious collection! You'll stay for the launch and the dealer presentations overseas where you'd better sell the collection well, but then I want you out of here. And I'll make it more than worth your while.'

She hissed in a breath, angling her chin higher. 'I already told you, I don't want your money.'

He stormed to the car, swinging his door wide open. Then he looked back at her standing there, his face a bitter mask.

'If there's one thing I've learned in business, it's that everyone has their price. Whores especially!'

His words ripped into her psyche, slashing her to her core as he reversed the car and accelerated away, leaving her as cold and shocked as if her lifeblood had spilled from the wounds and splashed out on to the ground.

After the story he'd told her tonight he would never believe the truth. It had suited her to never set him straight, but now there was no chance he would ever see her as more than his father's whore.

But he had a right to be angry with her. Wouldn't she feel the same way if someone had kept her a family member's final words from her? She'd failed in her duty to convey a promise. She'd let Laurence down, unable to honour either of his dying wishes. She hadn't passed on his apology. And by not doing so, she hadn't come close to taking care of him like his father had asked.

Two simple requests. She'd blown them both. How, then, could she hope to live up to Laurence's expectations of her in the business? How could she ever hope to work with his son again?

She couldn't.

'You win, Zane,' she whispered as the tail-lights of the departing car swung around a corner and disappeared from view. 'I'm leaving.'

It was like stepping from the wet season into the dry. She was in the office at five the next morning and, as soon as she'd sent the email to Zane confirming that she agreed to leave after her launch commitments had been honoured, it felt like the dark clouds had gone and the intense humidity had blown away. Soon there would be no more storms. And soon the air would be fresh and pure.

An unfamiliar sense of optimism filled her senses as she headed to the workroom to spend the morning making a final check of all the pieces in the collection, ensuring that any last-minute manufacturing changes had been made before signing off on each piece.

Because escape was at hand, escape that she'd hungered for ever since Zane had appeared on the scene, and an interview with the lawyers to put her parting arrangements in place was potentially only hours away. And if Zane wanted to press her with money to make her leave, she'd barely slept last night for working out the best thing to do with it. She didn't want it for herself, but it might as well go somewhere it was needed.

The bulk of it, she'd already decided, should go in trust to the employees. After all, if she was abandoning them then she'd make sure they were taken care of, maybe not quite as Laurence had intended, but in such a way that they would not be left completely to Zane's mercy. She'd get the lawyer to have the money invested with the employees as beneficiaries. Then, whatever Zane did, whatever became of their original ten per cent share, at least they'd have some guarantee of an income in the future.

The balance, the twenty per cent premium he'd offered for the shares, would go to the work her sister Opal was doing in Sydney. Pearl's Place, the women's refuge her sister had established, was expanding, driven by demand for its services. Ruby had always been too far away to help with Opal's work before, but now she would have the funds to help in a significant way. If she could achieve both these things without short-changing the employees, then wasn't her leaving doing good? Surely Laurence wouldn't hold that against her?

She turned the passion pendant in her fingers, feeling the burst of achievement that always accompanied seeing it. But this time there was another emotion mixed in. Sadness. It would be a relief to leave, but there was a sense of loss, too. The years she'd spent with Laurence had been wonderful. He'd taught her so much, he'd given her so much. But at least she could give him the Passion Collection, dedicated to his memory. It would be her final parting gift.

'I'm glad you've seen sense at last.'

She snapped up her head to find Zane filling her vision, his body language wearing his triumph like a prize, his eyes flashing victory. She swallowed back on an erratically beating heart. He wasn't the only one gaining something out of this. She was also a winner. She pushed herself higher on her stool.

'You got my email, then.'

He moved closer without answering and she swallowed, the air in the room noticeably thinner, the temperature suddenly rising.

So much for leaving behind the wet season, she registered as he moved to her side. She'd forgotten just how hot and stifling the dry could be.

'What's that?' he asked, looking down at the object cradled in her hands.

Instinctively her fingers closed protectively around the pendant—would he see what she'd seen inside it?—but then sense prevailed and she opened them, exposing the centre-piece of the Passion Collection to his gaze. 'The passion pendant,' she said. 'It's finished.'

He frowned, not believing what he was seeing. His gaze narrowed as he recognised the piece. 'This is the pendant you created for the collection? The one I saw as just a drawing?'

She nodded as he took the pendant, the heat from his hands brushing her skin like a warm glow. He held it up to the light, moving it around in his fingers, watching the play of light and shade on the surface of the gems, seeing the image within revealed.

The lovers' embrace!

Ruby had turned a concept into a reality, the experience of passion into a work of art. His skin prickled as the illusion winked back at him—the warm glow of flesh in the pearl nacre, the wonder of long golden limbs, entwined around those of her lover. It was passionate and provocative and it made him see all kinds of things—heated, forbidden, dangerous…

Then wonder turned to revulsion as reality interceded. Who was he kidding? The collection was to be dedicated to Laurence. Who had been Ruby's inspiration if not him? It was his father he was seeing, the remnants of their relationship, preserved for posterity, *no one else*!

He thrust the piece back into her hands and stormed to the door, his movements weighed down with need, heavy with self-recrimination. Oh, the collection would be a success, he had no doubt of that now, not if she managed to convey the same sense of passion throughout the entire collection.

But at least afterwards she'd be gone and he wouldn't have to deal with these constant reminders of her unavailability any more.

'Zane?'

He turned at her call. 'What is it?'

She frowned. 'The lawyer—how soon can we see him?'

With a jolt he remembered why he'd come to find her. 'Finlayson has taken leave. I didn't want to deal with his clerk about this.'

'So how long do we have to wait?' She sounded anxious, no doubt desperate to get away. Had she been thinking about the money after all, and about all the things she could do with it? He'd thought as much. How quickly she'd changed her tune.

'Relax,' he said, wishing he could take his own advice. 'He'll be back in a month. I've made an appointment for us both for his first day back on deck—the day after the launch.'

In a way it was easier working with Zane after that. They both knew what had to be done in the business leading up to the launch and they understood what was to come afterwards. Just knowing there was an end date on their working together made everything so much more bearable; almost like releasing the steam from the pressure-cooker situation they'd been trapped in together up until now.

Ruby threw herself into the launch and the plans to take the collection afterwards to Sydney and then on to the New York and London dealers. Zane had already decided not to accompany her on the overseas trip, although he planned to attend the Sydney show, so it was almost as if she would be escaping the business even earlier than she'd expected. She could hardly wait.

And it was wonderful to be able to concentrate her efforts on the design side of things once again and let Zane assume more and more of the management issues. Not that she didn't keep a watchful eye on what he was doing. She was still equal managing partner and there was no way he was going to run the business into the ground. But as the weeks went by she had to admit he had a real flair for the business and their arguments became fewer and farther between.

Preparations for the launch consumed days and weeks in a whoosh. When she wasn't going over the details, checking and rechecking everything to make sure the evening ran to plan, as the days counted down to the launch Ruby kept a nervous eye on the weather forecasts for the evening.

Timed to the minute, with a parade of the most spectacular pieces in the collection, the ceremony was set to conclude a scant five minutes before the rising of the full moon and the famed Stairway to the Moon phenomenon.

It was the one thing she couldn't control and she knew it was a risk. If all went well, the full moon would rise like a giant pearl over Roebuck Bay, its light catching on the damp tidal flats and building the appearance of a staircase rising up from the earth to the moon. Cloud cover would mar the illusion. A clear night would crown the evening's success.

Ten minutes before the first guests were due to arrive it seemed everything was in place. Ruby stood in the ballroom of the Stairway Hotel, looking out the large picture windows, scouring the sky for any trace of cloud and battling to keep her nerves in check. Never had a collection been so spectacular. Never had a collection meant so much. But would the audience see it that way? So much was at stake.

Behind her the staff were putting the finishing touches to the seating, tying colourful satin bows around them and preparing trays of champagne glasses.

'Looks like you got lucky.'

Zane appeared at her elbow holding two flutes of champagne. 'Congratulations,' he said, his voice deep yet strained as he offered her one. 'You've worked flat out on this launch. And you even managed to get the weather to co-operate.'

She looked back over the bay, allowing herself a smile in answer when all she really wanted to do right now was remember how to breathe. Zane was complimenting her? It was true that in the last few weeks since she'd decided to leave they'd formed an unsteady truce, but that rarely went beyond approval of budgets or promotional plans.

But that wasn't all that was threatening her ability to breathe. Some time since she'd last seen him he'd taken advantage of the suite they'd each been offered and changed into a crisp white shirt and a black dinner suit that made him look somehow darker and more dangerous than ever. His hair, freshly showered, clung in damp waves and he smelt good, clean and strong. *Intoxicating*. All of which she could have dealt with if not for the vibe emanating from him, a highly pitched tenseness surrounding him, setting her already strained senses to prickling alertness.

She flicked a glance his way, unsurprised to see him still watching her, only confirming what she'd felt so bone deep.

'I'm not sure if I need champagne right now. I think I need to keep a clear head.' Not that there was any chance of that while this humming tension surrounded her.

He took a sip, but it was the way his eyes drank her in that kick-started the low, fluttering heat deep inside.

'It'll relax you.'

I doubt it, she thought, even as she raised the glass to her lips, her senses heightening by the second as he brushed her arm with his as he raised his in a toast.

'To the launch,' he said, his eyes never leaving hers. She raised her glass in salute and drank again, not sure if it was the champagne already fizzing in her veins or something else.

'I think I'm too nervous right now to relax,' she admitted.

'Don't be,' he said. 'I don't know how you did it, but from the buzz going around it looks like the launch is going to be a huge success.'

If only she'd been talking about the launch. Ruby dragged her eyes from him and gazed out past the mangroves and across the flats. At high tide the sea would rush to fill the bay, transforming it a vivid blue, but for now, at low tide, only a narrow aqua ribbon of creek remained, bisecting the flats, a reminder of the colour to come with the returning tide.

It was almost like the change in Zane. This past few weeks he'd seemed so different; they'd worked together like a real team and, while he was giving her credit for the launch, he'd shouldered much of the load himself and she'd been more than happy to hand over responsibility. He could be such a different person to the man who'd hated her on sight. It was almost as if the tide had swept out on him, leaving a taste of the real Zane exposed beneath.

And tonight he was even more different, the air around him more highly charged, unsettling her, and causing urges to ripple through her that she had no right in feeling. It was easier when he hated her. It was easier, then, to hate him back. But now...

He could sense her tenseness. He could see it in the way she held her shoulders rigid. It emanated from her like a living thing. Tomorrow they'd see Derek Finlayson and sort out the terms of her departure and no doubt her tension would slide away—as it would settle things for them both. But that was tomorrow and right now Derek was no help to either of them and so the urge to reach out and massage her bare shoulders, to massage out the kinks, and soothe her troubled muscles, was almost overwhelming. She'd be gone soon, gone from Broome and gone from his life— What would it hurt to touch her? Just one touch of her honeyed skin, one chance to skim his hands over that satin perfection...

He hauled in a breath and clamped down on the urge, balling his free hand into a tight fist. He mustn't do it. He mustn't touch her. If he put one hand on her skin it would be too difficult to resist sliding the tiny shoestring straps down her arms, to kiss the skin at that place on her throat that betrayed the hitched beat of her heart, to peel away the gown that wrapped its way around her so tantalisingly.

The silvery pink gown hugged her form, her every movement giving light to the tiny sequins scattered between the shell-like shapes worked into the fabric, her hair gathered low at the nape of her neck to accentuate the strand of perfect pearls from which hung a small pendant from the Passion Collection, its design still voluptuous and evocative.

She blinked, the colour rising in her cheeks at his un-ashamed appraisal.

'You look beautiful,' he couldn't help but tell her. 'Like treasure from the sea.'

Her aqua eyes held with his, just long enough for him to admit the rest with his own— *I want you.*

Like a blow to the gut, that single truth forced the air from his lungs. There was no point denying it any longer. There was no point pretending. He wanted her.

And nothing would stop him having her.

The soundless words echoed in the heightened air between them before her attention was snagged by voices. Her eyes widened as she looked around him.

'It's showtime,' she said on a breath, depositing her near-empty glass on a side table.

Before long the place was humming and the formal part of the evening and the speeches got underway. Zane spoke briefly in his father's place, introducing Ruby and surprising her yet again by crediting her as the genius behind the collection. Then it was Ruby's turn. She took the podium and talked about the magic of working with pearls, in ancient times considered gifts from the gods and even the tears of the moon, and that was why she considered there was no better night than the full moon to celebrate the Passion Collection. Battling the prickle of tears, Ruby finally dedicated the collection to Laurence Bastiani's memory, recognising him as a man who'd pursued a dream and made that dream a reality for everyone to enjoy the most beautiful pearls in the world.

And then it was time for the collection to be unveiled. The

models paraded the catwalk, all of them stunning, all of them dressed to kill. But it was the pearls that the audience had come to see and it was the pearls that held their interest as, for all their beauty, the models were merely the backdrops to display the finest that nature could provide. Necklaces featuring pearls and tourmaline, long ropes of perfect golden pearls, bracelets rich with gold and voluptuous baroque shapes and earrings elegant yet bewitching—the crowd accepted each offering with mounting excitement, only to erupt in triumphant applause when the final piece, the magnificent passion pendant itself, was displayed.

It was too much! Tears, this time of success, filled her eyes. Someone squeezed her hand. *Zane*.

'Congratulations,' he said. Then he lifted her hand to his mouth and kissed her palm, the feel of his lips, the graze of his tongue on her sensitive flesh turning her liquid inside. 'Now go up and take a bow.'

Somehow she managed to negotiate the few short steps to receive a standing ovation from the audience, cameras flashing as the models embraced her.

Only the haunting sounds of a didgeridoo, the signal that the moon would soon be rising, could interrupt the excitement. Doors leading from the ballroom to a large balcony deck had been opened and the audience gathered drinks and filtered outside to the now darkened evening, their chatter still filled with awe at the collection while they kept one eye out on the horizon.

Zane handed her a fresh glass of champagne and steered her to their VIP seating.

The crowd had quietened, as if everyone was holding their breath in anticipation, the timeless music winding a spell around everyone, holding them enthralled as it seemed to beckon for the moon to appear.

And then behind the low hills across the bay emerged a tiny

pinprick of light. The crowd gasped collectively as all eyes focused on that one spot, as slowly the magnificent full moon emerged, bit by bit, bright and beautiful and so, so large.

Gradually, as it crept higher above the horizon like a giant pearl, its lunar glow illuminated the tidal flats with a shaft of golden light that slowly made its way down to the earth, step by golden step, until the stairway was complete. And there it was, a ladder, rising in front of them, so bold and vivid and real, a stairway to the moon.

He watched her profile, saw her expressions change and reflect the awe she was feeling at the spectacle, her lips slightly opened, her eyes bright and luminescent. Reflecting the awe back at him.

So many times he'd witnessed this phenomenon in his youth that he'd taken it for granted. But now, watching Ruby's features filled with wonderment, with the ancient sound of the didgeridoo heralding the occasion, it was like watching it for the first time. It was like suddenly understanding the magic. It was a moon made for lovers. Made for them. And he understood. He had no choice but to want her. Like the moon rising every night, it was inevitable.

In spite of everything he'd believed, in spite of the failure he was sure the collection would be, she'd captured the wonder of the illusion in her designs, she'd captured the beauty of the moon and all of nature with her pearls and he'd like to capture her with them, to wind them around her, to see them warm and lustrous on her flesh, and to tug her close with them.

'It's beautiful,' she said, leaning over towards him, her voice a breathless whisper.

'You are,' he agreed softly against her ear, her scent adding another dimension to the images, the hunger inexorably building inside him, becoming fraught with desperation. 'Very beautiful.'

He felt the tremor move through her, but she didn't pull away. He wrapped an arm around her shoulders to support her and after a second's hesitation felt her relax into him. Her skin felt warm and smooth and the tension she'd worn before the launch had been replaced with a melting languor in her muscles that only made him harder.

The moon climbed higher into the night sky and the staircase steps fractured and drew apart and the illusion slowly began to fade, the stairway transformed to a golden memory. People started talking among themselves and moving around, taking advantage of the finger food that had been laid on while they'd been watching the moon's brilliant display.

She made a move against his arm and sense told him he'd have to let her go. There would be photo calls waiting for her, interviews by the press, a world of people and clients to impress, further frustrating his need to be with her. But before he released his hold completely, he leaned over and nuzzled the warm skin under her ear. 'Later,' he whispered against her answering quake.

It was late. The guests had filtered away, the last of the reporters and photographers had departed and the moon wasn't the only thing that was high. Ruby had never felt more vitally alive, the blood in her veins a highly charged cocktail of success, adrenalin and two glasses of champagne. Nothing stood a chance of wiping the smile from her face tonight.

She turned to farewell the last guest, but it was Zane who folded her hand in his.

'Zane!' she said, practically glowing. 'Isn't it wonderful? The collection is a success.'

'It's a triumph,' he agreed, drawing her closer so she had to look up to him, close enough that his scent was welcomed into her senses like a missing ingredient. 'And you're the star of the collection.'

His words added to the intoxicating mix circulating in her veins. She had done well. But for Zane to acknowledge it…

'I'd also like to add my congratulations on your success tonight.'

'Thank you,' she whispered back, unable to turn her eyes away, even as his face drew slowly nearer. She watched his lips, hypnotised. She waited, feeling his warm breath melding with hers, wrapping around her, set to the music of her heartbeat. And then his lips touched hers, their pressure like a butterfly kiss, the feeling warm and sensual and their gentle movements across hers stirring ragged heat inside her, dissolving her bones, melting her resolve.

He pulled away till their intermingled breath was their only point of contact.

'It's late,' he said, his voice gravelly, his grip on her hands tight and urgent, 'and it would be crazy to drive when we have rooms already booked.'

She didn't want to drive, either. She was way over the limit, drunk on success, drunk on raw need, drunk on the danger she sensed she was in tonight.

All night long she'd found herself replaying the words he'd spoken to her over and over in her mind, lingering over them, tasting them—*'You look beautiful,'* he'd said, *'like treasure from the sea.'* And she'd felt so good, just the way he'd looked at her, and that had been before she'd felt the squeeze of his hand, the rasp of his tongue against her palm. That moment she'd come close to meltdown.

She looked up at him, still heady with accomplishment, reluctant to end the evening when it had gone so very well and when Zane had been so much a part of making it so. Maybe because his dark eyes were warmed to liquid, glossy with heat, like chocolate spiced with chilli, spicing up her own need, setting her thoughts to reckless.

'I don't plan on driving anywhere tonight.'

Sparks flared in his eyes, the tight line of his lips relaxing enough to turn up at the ends. 'Then I'll see you to your room.'

Just to her room? Or beyond? She shuddered at the pictures suddenly crowding her mind's eye, pictures of her with Zane, kissing her, undressing her, making love to her. Her breasts tightened and ached under her fitted bodice. Just the notion of sharing her bed with Zane turned her dizzy, her senses tingling. But this was Zane— What was happening?

She let him take her hand and lead her from the building, out into the gardens and the warm night air. He looped one arm around her shoulders as they strolled past the tumbling waterfall and swimming pool and through the stands of palm bushes, the air sweetly scented with frangipani, their brilliant white petals glowing softly in the moonlight. Halfway to their rooms she convinced herself it was easier to curve her arm around his back than to leave it awkwardly between them, and was immediately rewarded by the flush of contact, her hip brushing against his thigh, her breasts edging on his chest. He felt warm and accommodating yet still so tightly controlled under her hand, and she itched to pull back the layers of his clothes and find the source of that heat, to find the source of that control.

Lost in sensation she stumbled forward, her fine heel trapped between paving stones. He swung himself forward to catch her, his free hand missing her arm, cupping instead one breast as he arrested her fall. Her shoe jerked free behind her and she fell further into his hand, only straightening when she'd regained her footing. His hand gentled its hold and for a moment she thought he might remove it completely. But she was wrong. It lingered there, his touch now more like a soft caress than a lifesaver, the subtle movement of his fingers like a call to her need.

She looked up into his face, and against the soft moonlight his features were shadowed but intense. His dark eyes glinted with desire and his breath came like a low growl.

She lifted a hand to cover his—to take it away?—but if she'd ever intended to, then she forgot the moment her skin connected with his. She felt his hand touching her, she wove her fingers between his, she slid her fingers along and circled the band of his wrist as all the while he gently stroked her breast, and then she squeezed his hand—a silent supplication—that told him—*more*.

She didn't have to wait long for his answer. He caught her hand in his, quickly snared the other and wound them behind her, holding her captive, pressing her tight against him as his mouth descended upon hers. This time his kiss was different, deeper, more urgent, more testing. His lips were warm and he tasted of coffee and fine wine, of darkness and moonlight and she wanted to drink him in. His hands slipped down, cupped her behind and pulled her deliciously up against him. She gasped when she felt his power, felt his raw need, and all the while his mouth wove a spell on hers.

He drew his head to the side, raining tiny kisses up the line of her jaw. 'I want you,' he growled, his voice straining and urgent.

'I know,' she answered without hesitation. Because if she hesitated, she'd think, and she didn't want to think. Tomorrow there would be time for thinking, time for planning. Tomorrow there would be lawyer visits and settlements and no doubt a resurgence of the anger and resentment that had marred their first months together. *But this was tonight*. And tonight would be her only chance to live out the one fantasy that had preoccupied her dreams and snuffed out all others. She would have him, just as she'd long dreamed, if only for this one night.

He drew back and looked into her face, as if wanting to

assure himself that she knew what she'd just agreed to. But if he was surprised by her acquiescence, he didn't show it. Instead his eyes just glinted with approval. And without taking his eyes from hers, he swung her into his arms and swept her through the gardens.

He moved darkly through the balmy evening, her weight seemingly no trouble to him even as he climbed the stairs to the exclusive suites, the lines of his face chiselled in the soft moon glow. He could be a pirate, she thought, or a creature of the night spiriting her away. Tonight under the full moon, he could be anything.

And tonight she would be his!

CHAPTER EIGHT

'I MUST HAVE YOU!' he groaned, wheeling her around and pressing her against the closed door, his mouth crashing down on hers once more. Her lips parted under his sensual onslaught, welcoming the interplay of tongue and lips and mouth and skin.

He slid down the thin straps of her gown and swivelled her away from the door just enough to drop his hand behind her so her back arched towards him. He freed her breasts and groaned at their peaked beauty, muting the sound as he filled his mouth with one perfect breast, his tongue circling, tasting, his teeth toying with the hardened bud of her nipple before he set to work on the other peaked perfection.

His mouth was at her neck, back to her mouth, and the blood roared in his veins, pounded in his head, blotting out everything but the need. The need consumed everything. The need was everywhere, in his mouth, his hands, his skin. Then she writhed under him, pressing her belly closer against his erection and he groaned into her mouth. And that need—right there!

He wanted to make love to her. He'd imagined it, he'd pictured it, he'd fantasised about it for as long as he could remember.

But now there was no time to make love.

Right now he had to take her.

Her skirt frothed like sea foam in his hands as he rucked up her hem. Meanwhile her hands were in his shirt, under his shirt, sliding under his waistband, further inciting him. His hands reciprocated, circling her, releasing her from the scrap of lace fabric that was his final barrier. His hand cupped her mound, his fingers separating her, her slick wetness his reward but also his downfall. The urgent drumbeat of blood drove him onwards, prevented him from lingering where he would otherwise take his time, where he would later explore. But for now there was but one thundering imperative, one desperate, crashing need.

She clung to him around his neck, her arms wrapped tightly as he sucked her into his kiss while he freed himself. She tasted of sweetness and pleasure and everything he'd ever lusted for and any second now he'd feel that sweet perfection all around him and that knowledge powered him, urging him on. He lifted her, wrapping her legs around him, opening her up to him, and finding the core of her need and pressing himself, seeking entry to her tight honeyed depths, desperately seeking absolution from this driving need before he exploded outside.

'Please, now,' she cried urgently, her legs tightening around him, urging him home, and he responded, angling her closer and taking advantage of her slickness with one desperate lunge. The angle was better this time, he felt the resistance shift and give way and then he was in paradise—a frantic and frenzied paradise, powerful and passionate. Bliss.

Muscles clamped around him, Ruby's grip constricted around his neck and over his own rush of blood and heat he was certain he heard a scream—not of fulfilment, but of pain—and suddenly her tightness made sense. Horrible, chilling sense.

And paradise turned to hell.

* * *

His chest still heaving, his breath ragged, he withdrew, the need that had consumed him rendered insignificant in the pained knowledge of what he had done. He tugged her arms from around his neck and let her slide to the floor before he adjusted his clothing. Her lips were tightly pressed together, her mascara-smudged eyes clamped shut and aimed floorwards, moisture welling up from between the lids as she wrenched her dress up over her naked breasts.

'Why didn't you tell me?' Shock turned his heaving words into an accusation.

Her eyes opened and flashed cold fire at him. She swiped at her tears on her cheek with the back of one hand. 'And you would have believed me? I don't think so.'

'You let me believe you were sleeping with my father!'

'You believed what you wanted to believe! You decided it the moment we met and nothing I said or did was going to change that. You as good as labelled me his whore!'

He spun away, his mind in turmoil, hands clutching at the back of his neck. She was right. He'd had her pegged from the very beginning. And he couldn't have been more wrong. She couldn't have been his father's mistress. She was a virgin.

Had been a virgin!

She'd cried out in pain. He'd been so desperate to have her, so rushed he hadn't even waited to get her to the bed. It shouldn't have been like that for her first time.

He turned to see her retrieving her silky underwear from the floor. She'd adjusted her dress, slipped her arms back into the straps and straightened when she saw him watching her, balling the panties between her hands.

'Did I hurt you?'

No more than usual. 'Does it matter?'

'I didn't mean to hurt you. I didn't know…'

'I'm fine,' she said, when it was clear she was feeling anything but.

He took a step closer. 'Ruby—'

'Forget it! It was a mistake,' she said, turning for the door handle. 'I think we both realise that. It's just as well I'm leaving Broome soon.'

He crossed to her, punching the door closed before she could pull it open more than a few inches. All this time he'd assumed she'd been his father's mistress. All this time he'd been wrong! His father had never slept with her at all. And that made no sense, not with what he knew of his father. Not given the fact she'd lived with him!

'Don't go like this. Can't you see? This changes things—' He didn't know how, only that it must.

'This changes *nothing*!' she stated, her voice edging towards hysteria. 'It was a mistake, that's all. Tomorrow I'll meet you at the lawyer's office and we'll settle my departure arrangements, just as we planned, as if tonight had never happened, which I'm sure suits us both. And now—' She looked pointedly at his arm, still holding the door closed '—if you'll excuse me?'

He studied her, a muscle in his jaw popping as his eyes searched her face. She was right. It would be much better for both of them if they pretended this had never happened. He reached for the latch and swung the door open wide.

She must have been crazy to have gone along with him tonight! Safely in her room next door, she pulled off her gown and threw it on to the bed before pulling on new underwear and casual linen pants and a top. She yearned for a shower to wash the touch, the memory of him away, but she dared not, here. Just as she dared not cry. The tears had been perilously close in his room, his rapid departure from her like a slap in the face. He didn't want her when she was someone's mistress—he didn't want her when she was a virgin. When would she get it through her head—*he didn't want her*! It was her shares he wanted, shares he believed were rightly his.

Well, as of tomorrow, he'd have his precious shares!

In a rush of frantic activity she collected up her few possessions. There would be time enough for a long bath, time enough for tears later. Tears for all the mistakes she'd made tonight.

She'd believed she'd wanted him so much that it wouldn't hurt and she'd been wrong. Way wrong. Even now she ached, that part of her tender and pulsing.

She'd been wrong again when she'd hoped he wouldn't notice that she was so inexperienced.

But she'd made the biggest mistake of all in letting it happen in the first place.

Only one thing held her together. Tomorrow they'd see the lawyer and have the legalities of Zane's buyout of her shares taken care of. Then it was just a matter of weeks until she concluded her Passion Collection obligations and she'd be gone. She'd be free.

Escape was at hand and it had never felt so sweet!

She caught her reflection in the mirror near the door as she left and it stopped her dead. She had mascara smudged beneath each eye, her lips looked plump and swollen from the Zane's ministrations, and her smile—the smile she'd brandished tonight and believed would last for ever—had disappeared from trace.

For a man who'd just been on an extended holiday, Derek Finlayson looked exceedingly tense. Over his reading glasses he peered with undisguised concern at them both seated ramrod straight at opposite corners of his desk.

'What can I do for you both?' he asked. 'The note in my diary was quite vague.'

Zane looked sideways at Ruby, but she gave him nothing, clutching on to some kind of letter in her hands and looking steadfastly away from him, just like she'd ignored his presence since he'd arrived in Finlayson's office this morning. He'd arrived early, hoping to have the chance for a few minutes' private consultation first, only to find her already waiting. So she couldn't wait to leave Broome? Why didn't that give him the buzz of satisfaction that it should?

Only the shadows under her eyes were some consolation. So she'd lost sleep last night, too? *Good.*

'We'd like you to draw up some paperwork,' he said, turning his attention back to the lawyer. 'Ruby has decided to leave Broome after all. She's agreed to sell her share of the business to me.'

Derek Finlayson blinked slowly twice before looking across at Ruby. 'Is this true, Miss Clemenger?'

She nodded. 'I have the collection tour to finalise, but as soon as I return from New York and London in two weeks' time, I'd like everything to be ready for my departure.' She unfolded and handed over the paper she'd been holding. 'Here are my instructions for the proceeds of the share sale.'

Derek took off his wire-framed glasses and regarded the paper on his desk suspiciously. 'You're both sure about this, then?'

'Absolutely,' replied Zane emphatically.

'Even though we discussed that you both working jointly in the Bastiani Corporation is what your father intended, indeed, wanted?'

'It doesn't matter,' said Zane. 'This arrangement clearly isn't working and we both believe it's time to do something about it. I've offered to buy Ruby's shares at market value.'

Her head snapped around. 'What about the premium?

You mentioned a premium of twenty per cent. What happened to that?'

Air hissed through Zane's teeth as he felt his insides tumble and freeze over. *So it was the money all along!* All that talk about not wanting it. All that bluster and pretence that she didn't want anything. And here she was with a letter all prepared—her instructions for the proceeds!

So what that he'd been wrong about her being his father's mistress? Her gold-digger stripes were still boldly in evidence.

'And here was me thinking you weren't interested in the money. Any increase on twenty per cent? Could I tempt you perhaps with thirty?'

She glared back at him. 'You were the one who offered it. Surely you're not thinking about reneging on your offer, not—now?'

She stumbled over the last word, almost as if she'd been intending to say something different. He knew what it was, his mind had already finished off the sentence for her—*after what happened last night*!

Is that why she'd agreed to go with him—because she'd figured on earning that premium on her back? Anger spiked afresh into his psyche.

'Oh, dear.' Derek Finlayson interceded between the pair. 'This is no doubt a forlorn hope under the circumstances, but I do have to ask you both if there's any chance you might reconsider? Your father was very keen that you manage the business together.'

'I'm sorry,' Ruby said, turning her attentions to Derek, her voice soft but determined. 'We've tried to make this work, we really have. But the Passion Collection is just about completed and it's time for me to move on. And Zane has a good handle on the business now. I'm sure that's what Laurence was really concerned about, so I can't see any problems.'

'Besides,' Zane added, 'it's not like he's in a position to make us do something we don't want to. We control the business now.'

Across the desk the lawyer sighed. 'Well, I'm sorry it's come to this, very sorry indeed. But I'm afraid it's not quite as simple as that.' He opened the file, flipping the pages until he found the one he wanted. 'Ah, here it is. You see, when Laurence made the arrangements for his will, he did ask me to withhold one particular detail from you both.'

'What are you talking about?' demanded Zane.

Ruby frowned. 'Why would he have done that?'

'The settlement upon each of you of forty-five per cent of the shares of Bastiani Corporation, and the remaining ten per cent to the employees and staff, came with one condition.'

'What condition?'

Derek Finlayson peered from one to the other over his glasses. 'That in order for the employees and staff to receive their entitlement in the business, and in order for you to receive your inheritance, the two of you would have to manage the business together first for a period of at least twelve months.'

'Twelve months!' Zane exploded from his chair. 'Are you saying Ruby can't leave now? Even if I buy her out?'

'I do apologise. I know what a shock this must be to you both. I didn't agree with him, but Laurence insisted—he maintained that if you knew about this condition in the first place then you'd fight it from the beginning and it would never work. And I must admit, I was hoping you'd never have to be told. But this is the situation…' He took a deep breath and looked steadily at Zane.

'You aren't in a position to buy Miss Clemenger out because, until that twelve-month period is up, neither of you actually owns the shares to sell.'

'She can't leave?'

'Neither of you can leave the business before that time, not unless you want to forfeit your own and the employees' ten per cent share. So, I'm afraid, if you want to ensure people like Kyoto and others are provided for under the terms of Laurence's will, you're going to have to keep working together for another nine months.'

'It can't be true.' Her voice was barely audible. 'There has to be some way out of this.'

Zane looked across at her, shocked to see her face drained of all colour, her blue eyes large like waterholes in a bleached desert landscape, her anguish plain to see. Guilt twisted his gut and yanked it tight.

Because she was a fighter—he'd seen that time and again over the months they'd been together. She could have taken this in her stride under any other circumstances. She most likely would have relished the challenge.

But not after last night. No longer was she merely anxious to get away with her millions. Now she was desperate to escape from him.

Derek shook his head apologetically. 'I'm sorry, my dear. There's nothing more I can do.'

She shot out of her chair before he'd finished speaking, rushing from the room with a cry like a wounded animal.

'Ruby!'

'Miss Clemenger!' the lawyer said, rising to his feet, her letter held out in his hand.

Zane grabbed his jacket and snatched up the letter on his way out. 'I'll take it to her,' he said.

Ruby stopped running in the park across the road, dragging in oxygen in the shaded gardens in a desperate attempt not to throw up. Escape was such a fragile illusion. One minute freedom loomed large and promising on the horizon, fresh and clean and full of promise and so real you could just about reach out and touch it. The next moment it shattered into dust and blew away on the wind, leaving you locked in reality.

Locked in hell.

How could Laurence have done this to her? What on earth had he been thinking? And as for asking her to take care of Zane, she couldn't even take care of herself. Last night had proved that. She'd done the one thing she'd sworn she'd never do. She'd allowed Zane to practically undress her, pushing down her dress and removing her underwear and she'd allowed him to press himself into her until he'd broken through her final barrier.

But worse than that, she'd wanted him to!

She'd behaved like the whore he'd always believed her to be!

Shame turned her stomach again, shame and self-disgust that she had been a party to the act, and she leaned one shaky hand against a tree to steady herself, the other hand at her throat. How could she stay in Broome after what she'd done? How could she face Zane day after day and calmly talk business with the knowledge of what they'd done hanging over them like a dark cloud?

'Ruby!' Zane called from across the road.

She didn't answer, instead moving deeper into the quiet gardens, still battling to get her churning insides under control. She didn't want to be reminded of just who she was locked in hell with.

A few moments later he caught up with her anyway. 'Are you all right?'

She swung around to face him. 'What do you think? I've just learned that I'm stuck here with you for another nine months. Of course I'm not all right!'

'And you think I'm happy about it?'

She turned her back on him. 'I don't care what you think.'

'Don't blame me for what's happened! I haven't done this to you. Blame your beloved Laurence. He's the one who set up this crazy scheme.'

'Only because he didn't trust you! And who the hell could blame him?'

He tugged on her arm, wheeling her around so she could see the colour in his face, the dark fury in his eyes. 'I don't know what his reason was or whether he even had one. I've sure as hell tried to figure it out. But believe me, I'm just as unhappy as you about being stuck in this nightmare.'

'Don't touch me!' she said, yanking her arm free, rubbing her upper arm where he'd held her, her eyes spitting blue fire. Of course he wasn't happy about it. He'd hardly want her under his feet, reminding him of last night's disaster, holding on to shares and control of a company he wanted for his own. Well, she had a solution, at least for the short term. It would give her time on her own, time to think, time to let the humiliating scars of last night's fiasco heal over.

'The Sydney release is less than a week away,' she said, 'but I'm owed some leave. I'm thinking I'll leave a couple of days early. I can catch up with my family before I take the collection to the dealers overseas.'

'All right,' he said cautiously. 'I'll meet you in Sydney before the show.'

'No!' she protested, licking her lips. 'There's really no need for you to come. We've done the major launch here and I'm already doing the tour on my own. I mean, if we're going to be stuck together for months afterwards, maybe it will do us both some good to have some time apart—especially...'

His eyes narrowed as her words trailed off and she was grateful that at least he had the grace to look uncomfortable.

'All right. I'll stay here. But any problems— I want to know about them, immediately.'

Zane checked his messages and slammed the receiver down again, snarling. One message from his London office saying all was well, three messages from Anneleise asking him to please return her calls and not a thing from Sydney. She'd been gone two days already—surely something was happening over there that he should be informed about! He should never have agreed to let her go by herself.

But she couldn't wait to get away from him. She couldn't wait to get her money.

His back teeth ground together.

For a moment there, when he'd first discovered she'd been a virgin, he'd felt things could be different between them. He wasn't sure how—he'd misjudged her, and badly—but suddenly he was aware that the ground rules had changed and maybe, if he could somehow put things to rights, maybe there was a chance to do something more about this desperate need to possess her.

After all, she'd wanted him that night. She'd been like liquid silk in his arms, warm and lush and, oh, so ready. Oh yes, she'd wanted him, the way she'd kissed him, the way she'd opened herself up to him.

He wanted to believe she still wanted him.

Because despite everything, he sure as hell still burned for her!

But cruel reality shook those thoughts right away. It was money she wanted! Despite all her protestations, her panic when she thought she was missing out on the premium for the shares had highlighted her greed more starkly than anything.

Oh, she'd still get her money, she'd just have to wait a bit longer for it. Laurence had seen to that.

The telephone rang and he swooped upon it. *This time!* 'Ruby!' he announced, as if saying it would make it so.

'It's Anneleise,' purred the voice at the other end. 'And I have some wonderful news!'

He'd given up on hearing from Sydney when he finally left the office that evening, slipping on his jacket against the coolish breeze as he headed for his car. An unfamiliar rustle of paper had him reaching into his pocket. One glance at the open sheet was enough—Ruby's typewritten instructions for the lawyer. He'd forgotten to give it to her—not that it was any good to her now. He almost rolled it into a ball to toss away when some of the words he'd glimpsed jagged into his conscience. What was that about a *Bastiani Employees Trust*?

Curiosity got the better of him as he slid behind the steering wheel of his car and fired up the coupé's powerful engine. If it was about the Bastiani Corporation, it was his business, too. He had to check it out. He flipped open the sheet of paper, his eyes widening, taking in the details, working out the sums.

Then, like a poisoned cloud, horror descended upon him, cold, clammy and life-sucking. Horror that he'd misjudged her so badly, horror that he'd got it so wrong yet again.

She was taking none of the proceeds of the shares for herself. *None of it!* Fair value for the shares would be settled on the new trust with any premium paid by Zane for her shares to be donated to some women's refuge called Pearl's Place, in Sydney. No wonder she'd been so worried about the premium! She already had it earmarked for giving away.

He turned off the ignition, but there was no blessed silence, not with the drumbeat of blood in his veins and the blast of recriminations going on inside his head.

How could he have got it so wrong?

CHAPTER NINE

IT SEEMED HALF OF SYDNEY'S glitterati were at the Sydney Opera House to welcome the Passion Collection. It was another fantastic success, all the more special for Ruby by having her sister and mother in the audience, as once again the finale just about brought the house down.

If enthusiasm translated into dollars, this would mean a very good year for the Bastiani Corporation and Ruby could take a good deal of the credit, which was some consolation at least for her forced retention in the company.

But right now, accepting the audience's applause, her heart couldn't help but swell with pride. She'd done what she set out to do so long ago when she'd left Sydney for Broome with just a degree in design and a desire to make the most beautiful jewellery she could. And now she'd become a success in her own right, just as both her sisters, Opal and Sapphy, were successes in theirs. Perhaps one day she'd share her sisters' success in their love lives, too, though there was much less chance of that. So far Ruby had been an unmitigated failure when it came to men.

She bowed one last time, looking out over the crowded auditorium when a movement, unexpectedly threatening and potent, jagged her gaze. Her heart lurched and shuddered. It couldn't be… But a second glance only confirmed the worst.

Zane! Looking dark and dangerous and dressed to kill in one mouth-watering tuxedo. His dark eyes were the only un-civilised thing about him. She swallowed. Their mutual gaze caught and held across the room and electricity powered her senses, setting her flesh to tingling. *With abhorrence,* she insisted, pushing away her body's reaction. Abhorrence laced with irritation. Just what the hell was he doing here, anyway?

She stepped down from the stage as the applause contin-ued, spying Opal and their mother making their way through the crowd towards her. Nervously she looked around, but there was no sign of Zane before she was swallowed into her family's embrace.

'Ruby!' Opal cried as she threw her arms around her sister's neck. 'You're a star!'

Her mother followed suit. 'What a stunning collection. You'll have the whole of Sydney singing your praises.'

'Not only Sydney, all the world.' The rich Italian tones were a welcome sound.

'Domenic!' she shrieked as her handsome Italian brother-in-law picked her up and spun her around in his arms.

'Your designs are so inspired, anyone would think you are *Italiana, tesoro mio.*'

She laughed at his fond endearment—she knew no one but Opal was his treasure—but still she let him kiss her as he set her gently back on to her feet.

'It's so good to see you,' she said, speaking to all of them while she was still looking at Domenic's handsome face, their arms still linked.

She felt a hand on her shoulder, startling her with the posses-sive grip and setting her temperature to overdrive, but she didn't have to see the owner of the hand to know who it belonged to.

'Sorry to break up this happy reunion, but I really need to discuss something urgently with Ruby.'

She looked around at him. He seemed tightly wound, his features rigid and purposeful. 'Zane, what are you doing here? Has something happened back in Broome?'

He wasn't looking at her, he probably hadn't even heard her. Instead, he was staring hard at Domenic, the look on his face dark thunder. And Domenic was giving as good as he got. The two faced each other off like stags about to lock horns.

Opal broke the silence first. 'Domenic, didn't you hear the man? Ruby is needed. Let her go.'

Domenic's eyes didn't leave Zane's. 'Is that right, Ruby?'

'Everyone,' Ruby said, trying to focus while all too aware of the fingers splayed so possessively at her back, the heat stroking her skin, setting it alight under his touch, 'this is Zane Bastiani, my joint managing director from Bastiani Pearls. Zane, this is my family—my mother, Pearl, and my sister, Opal. And this is Domenic Silvagni, my brother-in-law, Opal's husband.'

If he felt like he'd been caught off guard, he didn't show it. Underneath his air of tension he was all charm as he acknowledged the women.

'Domenic,' Zane said as the pair finally shook hands, their eyes less war-like, though still wary, as if still sizing each other up. 'I recognise your name. Hotels, isn't it? I've stayed at Silvers Hotel in Paris—is that one of yours?'

His eyebrows lifted. 'So very far from home, I am indeed surprised. I would have thought you'd be more familiar with the Clemengers Boutique Hotels' connection, given your star designer's heritage.'

Zane shot her a look that would shatter marble, but she ignored him, promising to catch up with her family later on, before letting him steer her towards a quieter space.

'What's happened?' she asked, imagining some major problem back in Broome for him to come personally.

'Why didn't you tell me?'

She had trouble registering his words. Her body felt like one bundle of tingling nerve ends, sparking and shorting every time he touched her with his guiding hand, and keeping them all under control was more than she could handle. Even after what had happened, even after the humiliation and scorn, her body still craved his touch, yearned for it, welcomed it. She clamped down on the sensation. It was a form of madness and she wouldn't give in to it.

Instead she smiled at the guests, accepting their congratulations, as he led her outside the auditorium to somewhere they could talk. 'Tell you what?' she asked, her nerves brittle, anxious to be back in the safety of the reception.

'That you were one of *the* Clemengers.'

'You never asked,' she stated plainly. 'And you were having so much fun painting me that gold-digger shade you keep so handy.'

He grabbed her wrist, swinging her around so she had no choice but to look into his face. 'I didn't know.'

'Obviously. So you made it up!'

'I *assumed.*'

'Same thing!' she hissed. 'You fabricated a story to suit yourself and your own sad prejudices. I told you I didn't need your father's money and you never bothered to find out why. You simply chose to believe I was some gold-digging whore, out for what I could get.'

His eyes flared with anger, then swirled into the muddy depths of contrition.

'That's one of the reasons I came—to apologise….'

She looked pointedly down to where her hand was still held in his iron clasp. 'And this is your idea of an apology? How strange. Most people begin by saying they're sorry.'

'Hell!' He let her go, spinning away and pacing the passageway, his hands sweeping back the sides of his jacket to prop themselves hard against his hips. This wasn't going the way he'd planned, but the bombshell that she belonged to *that* Clemenger family was just more surprise in a long succession of surprises that just proved he'd been wrong-footed from the start. He should have known about her connections and, if he'd done more than just look at the photographs of her on his father's arm, if he'd taken the time to read the articles rather than just toss them into the bin all those years, he might have. At least that would have explained why she didn't need the money. And it might have meant something more than coincidence that his PA had booked him into a Sydney hotel bearing Ruby's surname.

A group of partygoers swept into the passageway, the air suddenly filled with laughter and gaiety and half a dozen expensive scents.

Once they'd passed he grabbed hold of her hand. 'Come on,' he said. 'We can't talk here.'

'The reception...' she started.

'I won't keep you long.'

He led her by the hand down the steps as she scooped up the hem of her gown in the other. Tonight she looked like a golden memory of the Roman Empire, her hair coiled around her face and collected into a pearl clasp at the back of her head, with matching pearl earrings and bracelet. Her dress was amazing, the amber fabric wrapped skilfully over one shoulder and tightly around her feminine curves to drape gracefully in folds at her feet. He got the impression that if he pulled in the right place, the material would unwind around her, spinning her out like a prize.

'So what did you want to say?' she asked at the foot of the stairs, pointedly removing her hand from his.

He sucked in a breath, gathering his thoughts as they

strolled along the harbour-line. The night was perfect for a winter's evening, balmy and mild and with barely a trace of the humidity he was starting to become accustomed to in Broome. The Harbour Bridge lighting accentuated its elegant span across the harbour and the office-tower lights and houses of the north shore reflected on the dancing surface of the water like glittering gems. And with her large aqua eyes questioning him, the loose coiled tendrils of her hair floating around her face in the light breeze, she made a stunning view infinitely better.

He ached to stop her and pull her into his arms and give life to the dreams that had tortured him since that night in Broome, dreams of completion, dreams of doing it right. But he had less right to do that now than ever. So, instead of telling her how beautiful she was or scooping her up in his arms, he kept right on walking.

'I was wrong,' he began. 'I was wrong about you from the start and everything I've done since then has only made it worse. And I am sorry. So sorry.'

She looked up at him, her brow knotted. 'And that's supposed to make everything all right, is it?'

'Hardly. I just had to tell you. I couldn't wait for you to get back from Europe. It was too important, especially after what happened...'

His words trailed off and they stopped side by side at the edge of the harbour, looking out over the dark water, watching the foaming trail from a ferry cut a swathe across the water.

'I was so very wrong about you,' he admitted. 'I doubted your talent, I doubted your motivation and accused you of everything I hated in a woman, and, to top it all off, then I had to hurt you physically.'

He raised his head to the heavens before continuing. 'You know, I was jealous of my father. So jealous that he had you.

So jealous of your relationship. And it drove me crazy, wanting you when I thought…'

'You thought I'd slept with your father.'

'I'm not proud of it! But is it so hard to understand? You were beautiful, you lived with him and he left you practically half the business— What else was I supposed to think?'

'You might have asked,' she suggested drily, 'instead of accusing.'

'Yes,' he admitted, nodding. 'You're right. But that night at the launch I wanted you so badly that it didn't matter any more, I had to have you before you went away. Just once, to have you. And I was so blindsided by wanting you that I didn't care any more about my father or who you'd made love to in the past— I was past caring. I just had to have you. But the joke was on me. You were a virgin. You'd never been with anyone, let alone my father.'

'I didn't want you to know,' she admitted. 'I was hoping you wouldn't find out.'

He turned towards her. 'But why? I was so fast—too fast. I hurt you.'

'Because I was so close to leaving Broome. It was better the way things were. It was easier to hate you that way.'

'I don't blame you for hating me,' he said. 'I was gutted when I thought you were only interested in the money from the shares. And then I found out why you needed that premium.'

She frowned, her head tilting in question.

'You left your instructions on Derek Finlayson's desk. I was going to return them to you, but I slipped them into a pocket as I raced after you. By the time I found them again you were already in Sydney. And I realised I'd made even more of a mess of it. I couldn't wait until you came back. I had to tell you how wrong I'd been and how sorry I was.'

They stood in silence for a while, each lost in their own

thoughts, the gentle harbour breeze caressing them like a soothing balm.

'I should be getting back to the reception,' she said, 'but thank you.'

He shrugged and nodded. 'There's just one thing I don't understand.'

'What's that?' she said.

'Why did you live in my father's house? I know I was wrong to jump to conclusions, but how did it come about that you shared a house with him?'

She hesitated. 'I guess it would seem odd. But it's a long story. Basically your father saved me.'

'How?'

She took a deep breath and began, speaking softly into the night air. 'I'd come to Broome, fresh out of design college and it was the first time I'd lived away from Sydney. New job, new town, new possibilities. I was so excited. One of my new colleagues lived in a share house with another couple and they were looking for a fourth person to share with. I could have lived alone, but I was keen to make friends.'

She sighed. 'He was always so helpful to me and I was grateful. He drove me to work to save catching the bus and he'd wait to bring me home, even when I was so involved in designing a piece that I'd forget the time. But he never got upset about it. And if I needed anything, any time, he'd offer to take me shopping or whatever.

'It was my other housemates that noticed first,' she continued, 'and they worried enough to mention it to me. At first I thought they were overreacting, maybe even a little jealous. I really believed he was just a nice person, he'd never so much as made a pass at me. But after a while I began to realise they might be right—if I wanted to go anywhere, anywhere at all, even just to the library, he'd be there. If I looked like going out, he'd insist on coming, too. And then someone else asked me out on a date....'

Already Zane felt like growling. Instead he angled his head so he could see her profile as she gazed unseeingly into the distance, and her gown draping softly and swaying seductively with the gentle breeze.

'What happened?'

She looked down at her clasped hands and took a deep breath. 'He went ballistic. He told me that I couldn't go, that he wouldn't let me. Well, I was getting pretty sick of this crazy infatuation of his by then—it was getting to be like living in a prison. I wasn't particularly interested in this other guy, I just wanted a change, to meet a new face—and when I told him to chill out, he told me that I was his and that nobody else would ever have me.' She paused and he saw her tense and shiver as the ghostly reminder of times past moved through her. 'And that's when I got really scared.'

Inside him the anger built. He could detect the fear in her words, even though she was doing her best to keep her voice even, and he had to fight the desire to sweep her into his arms and make it better.

'What about the police?'

'Oh, I'd tried. I'd called them from work and asked if they could help me, but their hands were tied, they said, until he did something concrete they could charge him with.'

His fingernails bit into his flesh. 'What about family? Did you ask them for help?'

She smiled. 'They were all so far away, and can you believe I didn't want to worry them? I know it sounds ridiculous now, but Opal was recently married with a baby coming and the other, Sapphy, was off in Milan setting the fashion world alight. Plus, we'd only just been reunited with our mother, after twenty years—it wasn't like I could really talk to her about anything, let alone something so personal. And both my sisters were so successful, I just couldn't bear the thought of going home a failure. Besides, I loved working with the pearls. I was determined to make this job a success.'

He turned fully towards her, not pretending any longer to be interested in the view. 'You'd never be a failure,' he said, slipping one hand down the curve of her cheek. 'You've proven that in spades.'

She pressed her lips together like she didn't believe it, but then she didn't pull away, either.

'Anyway, to cut a long story short, finally he did something really stupid and the police had something they could act on.'

His gut clenched. 'Did he hurt you?'

She didn't say anything straight away, but he didn't miss her screwed-up face or the sharp intake of air. Then, on a slow exhale, her features gradually relaxed.

'Not physically. But the experience scared me so much—I didn't think I could trust anyone again. He just wanted me for himself. So one day he must have slipped something into my drink, because I woke up in an old fishing hut, somewhere in the scrub outside Broome, that stank of old fishing gear and God knows what else. And it was so hot inside I could barely breathe. My other house-mates raised the alarm and still it took them a day to find me. I was never so pleased to breathe fresh air in my life. I was so scared....'

She took a deep breath.

'Laurence was shocked. He was one of my first visitors in hospital while they checked me out. He hated that one of his employees had done this to another—I think he felt betrayed by this guy—but also he felt responsible that this could have happened in his organisation. My sister and mother came to visit and Laurence put us all up in his house, but after they'd gone home, I didn't want to stay by myself, so when Laurence suggested I stay until I felt more comfortable, I jumped at the chance.' She pushed herself up from the balustrade and swung around to face him. 'It might sound funny, but we'd been working together by then for almost a year and I did trust him. I respected him for his work in the pearl industry and he was teaching me so much. And I knew he valued and respected my work. He was probably the only person in Broome I could trust at that stage. My own father had died a few years before, and Laurence was a better father than he'd ever been.

'So you see…' she looked up at him and smiled '…your father rescued me. He made me feel safe when I was scared. He treated me like a treasured daughter. Can you now understand why I loved and respected him so much?'

Zane shifted uncomfortably in the late-night air. This wasn't the father he'd left, the father he'd damned all these years. She trusted him implicitly, the man he couldn't trust himself. Why was that?

And why was it that his father had been the one to rescue her when all Zane had done was to give her grief?

'You stayed with him all those years. Were you that scared that you wouldn't move out?'

'No. After a few months, once I knew the guy was safely locked up behind bars, I looked for an apartment, but it was right about then that Laurence had his first attack. It was only angina to start, but I couldn't leave him then, not when he needed someone with him. Kyoto was wonderful, but it would have been unfair to rely on him.'

The knot in Zane's stomach twisted tighter. Laurence's heart condition must have gone on for years and his father had never given him so much as an inkling. And Zane had never taken the time to find out how he was—he'd just assumed his bull of a father would last for ever. Grief and remorse swamped him. Why hadn't his father told him?

Why the hell hadn't he bothered to find out himself? How could he have let anger and bitterness so infuse his life that it permeated his every action?

'I'm sorry,' he said. 'I couldn't have been more wrong.'

It wasn't purely his fault, she knew, even though she hated the labels he'd pinned on her. But she'd let him believe what he had, choosing to put up with his antipathy rather than furnish him with the truth because it had suited her. It had been her defence, bolstering her own suspect resistance.

She could tell him that now—or she could leave it. They had months to live with each other after this, after all. It wouldn't make things easier if he had any idea how much she'd been affected by him from the start.

'I really should get back to the reception, now. If there's nothing else?'

He looked at her strangely, his face a complex blend of emotions. 'Actually, there is,' he said at last, as if he'd been weighing up whether or not to tell her. 'For what it's worth, I finally worked out what Laurence was doing when he set up his crazy bequest.'

She angled herself closer, curious. 'Surely he did it to ensure continuity in management and a way to ease you back into the family business?'

'I have no doubt that was part of it. But being Laurence, he had in mind a much grander plan. I think he was hoping we'd end up married.'

CHAPTER TEN

'YOU HAVE TO BE KIDDING!' she cried. 'That's just daft.'

'Is it so crazy?' he contended. 'Or is it just so obvious that neither of us thought of it before?'

'What do you mean?'

'Why else would Laurence leave us both forty-five per cent of the company? He'd never want ownership split that way permanently. But together we own ninety per cent. Don't you see—that must be why he asked Finlayson not to let us know about the twelve months' condition! He didn't want us to fight against his bequest from the start, each resenting the condition. He was hoping our long-term partnership would happen naturally, without being forced.'

'But to marry?' She was shaking her head. It was too fantastic, too far-fetched.

'Why not? What good would it do the business if we both up and left after twelve months? We'd have our share of the business, but who would run it? Or if I took off back to London? I know you could run the business, but when would you have time to work on your designs?

'But if we were married,' he continued, 'he'd have ensured the management base of the company into the future. Not two separate parcels of forty-five per cent, but combined almost a full ownership. So he arranged to put us together for twelve months. He gave us the shares, the conditions, the incentive of looking after the staff so that you wouldn't back out of it before your year was up. The rest he left up to us.'

It was insane. She was still shaking her head, signalling her denial of his crazy claims with every cell in her body.

'Why would Laurence do that?' Although, even as she asked, she was remembering his dying words. '*Look after Zane.*' Could marriage have been what he'd intended all along?

'Laurence was looking to build a dynasty. He'd already built the biggest and most successful pearling operation in the world, but his only heir had walked out on him. There was no way he was leaving its future to chance—he had to get me back and Laurence no doubt thought you'd be a good match for me. He was clearly proud of his protégée designer. Maybe he saw you as someone not only to lead the business into the future, but also to lure the prodigal son home?'

'If he was so into control, why wouldn't he have just made it a condition of the will that we were to marry to inherit, then?'

'Because he knew or suspected that we were both as strong headed as he was and that we'd never have gone along with something so proscribed. In my father's strange way of thinking, this was subtle manipulation.'

She brushed both his suppositions and his arm away with the same irreverent sweep of her hand. 'And now you're giving credence to this bizarre theory of yours? I simply can't believe you'd endorse anything that smacked of having your father's hand in it. In fact, I'd have expected, the way you feel about him, that you'd run a mile from anything you thought he was trying to manipulate you into.'

A muscle in his cheek twitched dangerously. 'We have learnt something about each other while we've been together.

As you say, I had that exact reaction at first. And then I got to thinking... There are worse ways to be manipulated.'

'I can't believe you're serious. Are you so desperate for control of my shares that you'd actually consider marrying me?'

'Why do you think this is about the shares?'

'What else would there be in it for you?'

He smiled uncertainly and came closer, the reflections of the walkway lights adding to the fire in his eyes, his movements measured and predatory, like some dark animal about to pounce.

'*You.*'

Oxygen!

She needed oxygen to get her mind to work, to power her muscles into action—into escape. But there was no oxygen left to power her thoughts or her body, it had all been burned up in the fire storm of his approach.

'I wouldn't blame you if you never wanted to see me again. But all I've dreamed of since you left Broome is to have a second chance with you, to make up for the mess I made of things and to make love to you properly, the way it should have been done. The way you deserve to be made love to.'

She swallowed back on a lurching heart while his eyes drank her in, feasted on her and then suddenly she was in his arms and it was his mouth, his hot mouth, devouring her and she was back in Broome, back in the hotel room, the same sensations, the same passion that had swept her away that same night with no thought to the consequences.

His hands circled her, pressing her tight up against him, reminding her starkly of what they had almost shared. She clung to him, feeling her body mould to his, her muscles strangely weakened and yet her senses empowered at the same time.

Because she wanted him. She wanted to feel him fill her once again. Her body hungered to feel him deep inside her. Her body craved the completion she'd been cheated out of before.

And he wanted her. Now he even talked of marrying her. Could that mean he felt something for her amidst all that?

His hands swept up the curve of her spine, rounded her shoulders and cupped her face as his kisses slowed.

'I want you,' he whispered. 'And I need you, tonight.'

She shuddered into his heated embrace as his words re-iterated his body's communication. 'But...' she said, trying to think when all she could do was want. 'But maybe I should get back to the reception.'

One hand moved, like a heated flow of ecstasy, down her jaw to her chest, cupping one breast in a warm embrace, brushing over her nipple in a way that made her dizzy with need.

'I know. But I need you. Now!'

It was a giddy journey back to the hotel. Giddy and hot and lightheaded. She was aware of his hands on her, holding hers, stroking her back, holding her tight at the waist, and yet, for all the innocence of how this might have looked to the casual passer-by, it felt like something else completely. Because nobody else could see the intent that accompanied his grip, nobody else could feel the electric hum of desire that coursed from him to her and back again.

Clemengers Hotel lobby was always marked by calm efficiency, but at this hour the atmosphere was even more hushed and discreet. Without asking, he led the way to his suite, never taking his eyes off her or letting his hands stray from her, never giving her one opportunity to back out. But she wasn't going anywhere. Not without Zane.

Because she was hungry for him and hungry for more of what he could provide, as if what had happened in Broome had been the entrée, teasing her appetite to critical levels, and tonight would bring the main course. What had she missed out on that night? Whatever it was, she was going to find out and more.

'This time, I'll do it right,' he whispered once they were safely inside the darkened room and something inside her swelled and bloomed. He raised her chin and kissed her lips and this time she sensed something new in his kiss, a tenderness, a taste of something deeper than desire. Commitment? Did it mean he really believed this crazy theory of his?

Then his fingers stroked the fabric covering her breasts and she gasped into his mouth and forgot how to think, giving herself up to the sensation as he trailed tiny kisses down her throat, covering her bare shoulder with his lips, easing his fingertips under the neckline of her gown. Already her prickle of arousal was turning into a rush of need.

'Such a beautiful gown,' he said, letting his fingers explore further, sliding them between the fabric and her skin, capturing one breast, his fingers ministering to it, worshipping it like it was a prize. 'But right now…' he smiled down at her, his eyes warm and filled with longing '…I want you out of it.'

Her breath stopped as he picked her up in his arms and carried her to the large king-sized bed in the bedroom adjacent. Once there, he kissed her again and deposited her gently, almost reverentially, on the soft cover of the bed. He moved to the windows and slid open the heavy curtains, letting the room fill with the soft glow of the harbour at night.

Then he turned back and looked at her and the world stood still.

Seconds were consumed, or it could even have been minutes, in the heated glow from his eyes. Like a flame it lapped at her skin, surrounding her in its warm embrace.

He shrugged off his jacket, threw it over a chair, pulled the end of his tie and tugged it from his collar and let it fall to the floor. Buttons were flicked through, one by one, as slowly, deliberately, he stoked up the fires. She swallowed, her mouth

ashen, her body tingling, as she propped herself up against the
pillows, flicking off her heels and tucking her legs beneath her.

If that night in Broome had been hurried and over too
quickly, then obviously this night was to be slow and languid.

He undid the buttons at his wrists, his eyes never leaving
her, and her eyes were drawn to the cleft in his shirt, to the
olive skin, and dark curls hinted at below until she ached to
reach out and touch him. Then he tugged free his shirt tails
and, as if he'd heard her silent pleas, walked to the bed and
sat down alongside her, so close that she could feel his desire
curling into hers, meshing with her own.

He wound a hand around her neck and drew her face to his
mouth and kissed her. Languidly. Deeply. She reached a hand
between them, slipped it under his shirt and felt his rushed
intake of breath as she explored the sculpted form below, en-
countering the tight nub of a nipple, running her nails through
the spring of chest hair.

Emboldened, hungry for more, her other hand followed
suit, drinking him in with her hands, from the tight lean
abdomen to his broad shoulders. Impatiently she scooped the
shirt over his shoulders, wanting more, and he obliged by
wrenching it down his arms and tossing it to the floor. There'd
been no time for such exploration before and she revelled in
it, luxuriated in the masculine tone of his skin, the coarse hairs
over the sculpted muscles.

He pulled back, his breathing rough, his eyes turbulent.
'Like I said—' his voice was gritty and low as he traced his
fingers under her shoulder strap '—we need to get this off.'

It seemed such a blur after that. There were so many sensations, so many discoveries, so many rewards. He slid her
dress down, she pulled through his belt, he peeled away her
stockings and she released him from his silken pouch until
finally, gloriously, both were naked.

He pulled the clasp from her hair, letting it float around her shoulders as he lowered her down among the pillows. In the low light her skin shimmered and gleamed, satin smooth and as rich as the nacre of a pearl, and as much as he ached to bury himself inside her, as much as he burned with need, after what had happened before, he knew that this moment was too important to rush.

He touched a hand to her face, stroking it down her neck to where another pendant from the Passion Collection lay against her skin, the design staggering in both its simplicity and its powerful suggestion. 'Beautiful,' he said.

Her hand reached for the heavy pendant and she lifted her head. 'Should I—?'

'Take it off? No,' he said, inspiration hitting him in that instant. 'Wait…'

He swung off the bed and padded across the room, his body magnificent, a study in shadow and light and such raw masculine power that she caught her breath, shuddering with anticipation for what was to come.

He reached into his jacket. *Protection*, she assumed with relief. Thank God one of them was thinking tonight. She'd long ago given up. And then he was back, something small deposited on the bedside table with a rustle and something else in his hands.

'What are you doing—?' she asked.

Cutting off her protest, he drew out a long rope of pearls and lassoed it around her neck, draping it in between her breasts, catching one wrist in a loop that travelled over the feminine curve of her tummy and down lower, much lower, where they kissed the whisky spring of curls.

'I borrowed it from the collection,' he admitted. 'I had this dream about you adorned with pearls. And pearls must be worn or without contact with the skin they fade and lose their lustre.'

She was just about breathless as the pearls went to work, stroking her skin like a thousand fingers, but warm like living things, moving against her skin like nature's caress.

'They were worn just this evening.' Her voice sounded strange to her ears, husky and tight.

'Not like this, they weren't.'

He leaned back and surveyed his work, his eyes glinting and hot with appreciation. 'Perfection,' he said. 'My treasure from the sea.'

And then his mouth was on hers, his body within heated proximity alongside, his hands exploring her feminine form, worshipping her, setting her body alight. And every time she moved her hand, the pearl rope shifted, rolled, tantalised, tugging at her senses, magnifying the experience.

He drew back, taking a loop of the rope and coiling it around her breast and then he dropped his mouth on to her peaking nipple, laving her, suckling her so that her back arched, driving her further into his mouth. First one breast and then the other, driving her wild, separating her from a woman with thoughts and plans and career to simply a woman of need, desperate pulsating need.

Then his mouth dipped lower, following the line of pearls on her flesh, tracing its path down her body. He kissed the tiny swell of her tummy, the scoop of her flesh that fell away from her hip bone and, when he parted her, she knew she was lost. One touch of his fingers, one flick of his tongue and she came apart, her body fracturing around him, absorbing him.

And just when she thought it could get no better, that she was on her way down from the most spectacular high she'd ever had—he entered her, in one long thrust that arrested her fall and took her up again. This time there was no resistance, no pain, only the welcoming build of intensity; with each thrust he took her higher, ever higher, building the pressure all over again, urgent and pressing as her body welcomed him, enclosed him, sought to retain him. And between them the pearls gleamed against her damp skin, moving as part of her, capturing the rhythm only to still at that point of no return, that point that preceded her plunge once more over the abyss.

But this time she wasn't alone.

He unwound himself from her arms and eased away for a minute, his body slick and spent, his breathing ragged, his mind and senses blown away. Never before had he found a woman so responsive. Never before had he come so totally undone. He turned and looked at her, struck by her beauty now more than ever, her hair wild in abandon on the pillow, her lips plump and pink and thoroughly kissed and a mantle of pearls whose beauty didn't come close to matching their wearer's. She could be a painting by Botticelli, a goddess emerged from the sea, a modern-day Venus.

Her eyes fluttered open. 'Zane,' she whispered in a way that made his insides curl.

He loved the way she responded. Already he wanted more, wanted to press himself into her, feel her tightly encased around him. He moved back to the bed, dropping his mouth to her breasts, alternately teasing them with the pearls and then his lips and teeth, loving the feel of her in his mouth, loving the taste of her.

He gasped when he felt her soft fingers brush against him, taking him by surprise. He held his breath, willing her to touch him, to cradle him in her hand, but what she answered with was completely unexpected. He growled with pleasure as coils were wound around him. He responded the only way he could, by hardening even more, filling the pearl coils even tighter, reminding him of another sweet, tight place....

'You're playing with fire,' he warned her.

'I want you again—now.'

He choked back a gasp as she tugged, tightening the noose still further. 'And you think that's the way to get me?'

'I think so,' she said, smiling up at him even as she applied more subtle pressure to her pearl lasso.

'So who said you're the boss?' he jibed, dipping his mouth to her nipple once again and studiously ignoring the urge to fill her right now. 'I thought we were supposed to be partners.'

'I never said you couldn't come, too.' Then she tugged at the pearls in such a way that they uncoiled around him in a whoosh. 'I need you—inside me—now!'

It was all he could do to focus long enough to prepare himself before plunging once again into her welcoming depths.

She was a witch, a sea witch, and right now what he needed was more of her magic.

It was a new day. A brand new day. A fizz of excitement zipped through her as she stood out on the tiny balcony, concentrating the sparks in places and muscles already protesting their overuse. Last night had been fantastic, mind-blowing and a revelation.

As for regrets? How could she have any? Zane was an amazing lover, he'd proved that so many times last night she'd lost count. And he'd made her feel so special, so precious. He'd wanted to do it right for her, and he had.

He'd felt so right.

Across the harbour the colours were changing and the new sun lit up the city coming to life. She sighed. What would Laurence really think? Had this been something he'd wished for all along, that they become a partnership in more than just their shareholding?

She smiled as she watched the pink sky wash away to grey and then blue. There was no guilt. Somehow she knew Laurence would approve. And somehow she suspected

Laurence knew she would fall for him. After all, Zane was his son—how could she not love him, too?

Love him?

She trembled in the early morning cool, pulling her plush hotel robe more tightly around her even as the first warming rays of sunlight washed over her. *She couldn't love him.* Not Zane. Not after everything that had happened between them. And yet…there was something that moved inside her that couldn't be ignored. Something that had his name inscribed on it.

He wasn't the complete villain she'd painted him from the start. Just as he'd assumed the worst of her, she'd misjudged him, too. And at least now she had some inkling of why he'd believed the things he had.

But could she be falling for him? Could she really be falling in love with Zane?

How could that have happened?

He stood silently, watching her standing wreathed in light, a beam of sun catching on the silken highlights in her hair, the sculpted perfection of her features.

Even the sun wanted her. Even the sun marked her as the one.

What was she thinking as she gazed out over the bay? Why had she abandoned his bed? Was she suffering morning-after regrets? He wasn't, that was a certainty.

As if suddenly aware of his presence, she turned her head. Her eyes widened and then she smiled that smile he'd first seen that day on the boat coming back from the pearl farm, that smile he'd wanted to see again, the smile he wanted to see made just for him. And just like that time, it was incredibly sexy. It lit up her face just as it stoked his fires. He knotted the loosening towel at his waist tighter and walked up behind her, wrapping his arms around her and burying his face in her neck.

'You're up early,' he muttered against her throat.

'And you're…*up*,' she acknowledged, wiggling her bottom tantalisingly against him.

He laughed, or rumbled more like it, a sound filled with intent as he pulled her back inside the French doors where the sun could still capture her, but they were safe from other eyes.

He kissed her sensitive mouth as he eased her up on to the marble side table, pushing in between her legs.

'Maybe you could help me with that,' he suggested, sliding her tie undone. She trembled as he drew her robe apart and slid his arms around her waist to catch her behind.

'I'm claiming you,' he said. 'Just like I claimed you in the night, I'm showing the morning that you're mine.'

His towel dropped from his hips and with a thrill of pure pleasure her eyes took in the magnificent fullness of him. She felt him nudge against her until every part of her was waiting, wanting, anticipating, and then he was pushing himself into her, taking her in one long, slow, sensual slide.

Filling her.

Impaling her.

Claiming her.

Instinctively she wrapped her legs around his waist and took him deeper until he pierced her heart. Had he meant what he'd just said? Because the primal rush she'd felt when he'd appeared, naked-chested, with just a white towel lashed around his hips; the primitive urge to mate that she'd felt when he'd pressed into her; even the feel of his body now cocooned in hers—they were nothing compared to the thrill of hearing him say that he wanted her, that he was claiming her for his own.

His words heightened his love-making, turned joyfulness to bliss, and when she came, as he pumped his release into her, there were four words she read clearly written amid the fireworks-lit heavens of the new day.

I love you, Zane.

CHAPTER ELEVEN

ZANE EMERGED FROM THE BATHROOM, already in a suit and tie, shaved and perfectly groomed, ready for his flight back to Broome. The mere sight of him caused her breath to catch, the hint of mischief in his eyes and his turned-up mouth turning her flesh to a slow sizzle. But he'd be out of the suite in less than five minutes, and still they'd not had a chance to talk. What would happen when she returned to Broome?

'We haven't had much of a chance to talk,' she said, nervously sipping on an espresso she was praying would lend her its strength.

His wicked smile turned up another notch, his eyes looked like they were peeling the robe from her. 'Not that we wasted a minute of the time we had.'

She blushed with the intensity of his gaze. 'At least we can forget about all those crazy ideas about marriage now, I guess?'

'Forget about it? Why the hell would we want to do that?'

She blinked, hope meshing with confusion in a tangle of thoughts inside. Why would he still want to go ahead with it? Unless...

Unless he felt something for her, too. Something beyond physical need.

She tried to laugh, to belie the tension she was feeling. 'So why would you seriously consider it? It's not as if you have to go to the trouble of marrying me to get me into your bed.'

'Who says marrying you would be any trouble?' he said, downing his tiny cup of coffee like a shot.

'Zane, be serious!'

'I am serious. I can't see what your problem is. We know we're compatible. We share a business and we've shared a bed, *most* satisfactorily. We've got more going for us than most people. And it appears we have Laurence's blessing. Your mentor. The person you admired and looked up to, more than anyone in the world. It's what *he* would have wanted, after all—to have you as his daughter-in-law, to provide him with more heirs. You don't want to let him down.'

She swallowed, her mouth suddenly dry and scratchy again. Right now this wasn't about what Laurence wanted. 'Well, then, what about love? Shouldn't love have something to do with it?'

His brow drew down a fraction, but then he just sighed and dropped an arm casually around her shoulders. 'It's not compulsory, if that's what you're worried about. I'm sure we'll develop some form of deep-seated affection over time. In fact, that's probably preferable to love.'

She reeled at his words, but at least he'd cleared up one question for her. He didn't love her. He might never. 'How can you say that?'

He shrugged. 'I know that love didn't help my mother. She worshipped my father, for all the good it did her. He betrayed her, just the same. She loved him more than anything and yet still he could abuse that trust and love and take a mistress. So maybe it's better not to love. Maybe it's better to save the emotion for the bedroom.' He planted a kiss to the back of her neck. 'We'll no doubt need it.'

If his last comment was an attempt to warm her after the

rest of his cold words, it failed miserably. She turned away and rose out of her chair, appalled, sickened by his cynical words. So what did that say for her love? What good was that to her if he felt this way? How committed would he be to her if he didn't love her—if he didn't ever expect to? Would he, too, expect to have his interest on the side, like he claimed his father had?

No, she couldn't bear that!

'Your father loved your mother. I know he did. He was devastated by her loss.'

'If he really loved her, he would never have taken a mistress! He would never have elevated her to the position she occupied.'

She shivered and crossed her arms over her chest, the force of his bitter resentment erecting a solid wall between them, reminding her of all the reasons why such a marriage could never work. 'I don't even know why we're talking about this. We don't have to get married. It's not as if it's a condition of the will.'

'Laurence clearly expected it.'

'You don't know that! Not for sure. And, frankly, I think you're wrong to even imagine that a marriage could work when there's no love involved.'

'Why? Can you honestly say that love was instrumental in your own parents' relationship?'

'I know that my father's lack of it was instrumental in their marriage breakdown!'

He hesitated, his head tilted, as if assessing the import of her words. Then he stood and crossed to where she was standing, putting his hands on her arms.

'Okay, maybe I'm rushing it. We have another nine months together before we have to do anything. Meanwhile, you'll be away for a week. Take your time—think about it while you're gone—and when you come back we can talk about it again.'

Then he kissed her one more time and headed for the door. 'Promise me you'll think about it?'

She nodded as he left. She'd think about it, certainly, not that it would do him much good. She could never marry him, not with his prejudice against his father, not with his cynical view of love and marriage. It just wouldn't happen.

'So tell me about Zane?'

Ruby looked over her cup of coffee suspiciously. When Opal had suggested getting together in her apartment for a chat, Ruby had suspected it wouldn't be too long before the fishing expedition got underway. 'Deft change of subject, big sister. I thought we were talking about how the hotel business is going.'

Opal laughed, scooping up her dark-haired, twelve-month-old toddler on to her knee and giving him a sandwich finger to munch on while four-and-a-half-year-old Ellie sat quietly on a rug, flicking quietly through a stack of books. 'Give a girl a break!' Opal pleaded. 'I live in a hotel. I work in one. I go to bed counting hotels instead of sheep. I'd much rather talk about a hot-looking guy any day. And you have to admit, Zane is one hot-looking guy—especially given the way he looks at you!'

Ruby put her cup down. Zane was no doubt already halfway back to Broome by now and tomorrow she'd be flying on to New York. Thinking time, she'd figured, intending to mull it over in her own mind during the long flights, but maybe it would be good to discuss it with her sister, first. Her emotions had been on so much of a rollercoaster ride since Zane had appeared on the scene, she could do with a fresh perspective.

'What exactly did you want to know?'

'You know, all the good stuff. What's he like? Is he a good kisser? And exactly how serious is it between you guys, anyway?'

'Who says I know how he kisses?'

Her sister grinned at her too-fast rebuttal. 'Well, you were missed at the reception last night—until someone spotted you both out on the promenade.'

Ruby felt her colour rise and turned away. 'So, it was just a kiss. That doesn't mean there's anything going on.'

'You have to be kidding! You saw how he acted last night when he showed up, the way he looked like he wanted to tear Domenic limb from limb for just touching you! That guy is seriously hooked.'

Ruby sipped her coffee and thought back to when she'd introduced the two. Is that what had been going on? She'd been so assailed by conflicting emotions and sensations, from the tingling awareness when Zane had arrived, to the shock when he'd taken hold of her shoulder and the huge satisfaction when Zane had realised her connections. There had been so much happening that she hadn't been able to make sense of it all at the time. Could Opal be right though? Had Zane really been jealous?

Mind you, what if he had been? It meant nothing more than that he wanted her in his bed and he was willing to face down the competition. It was pointless reading any more into it than that, no matter what she might have wished for.

'So,' Opal continued, handing little Guglielmo another tiny sandwich, 'how do you feel about him?'

She sighed. 'Confused,' she replied honestly, trying not to think too much about the night she'd just spent in his arms, the joy of being joined with him, the bliss at the way he made her feel and then the hollow emptiness of the uncertainty that followed. The harsh light of day wasn't just a cliché, it had become a reality.

'I really wish I knew. We couldn't stand the sight of each other at first. I hated the way he'd seemingly abandoned his father and he hated the closeness I shared with Laurence. But as for now—sometimes I think he might be the most special man on earth, but at other times…' She hesitated. 'At other times, I'm not so sure. Sometimes he can seem so angry and I don't know how he can ever get over it.'

'Angry with you?'

'No. He's angry at Laurence. He's bitter about his mother's death and it colours his view of so many things. He says his father had a mistress all the time he was married, apparently his wife's closest friend. It seems it was the mistress driving the car in which they were both killed.'

Opal's eyes opened wide. 'My God! And I thought our family had a bizarre history. But you knew Laurence well— what do you think?'

'I can't believe Laurence would betray a trust that way. He was a man of integrity. I'm confident that the Laurence I knew would never do such a thing.'

'Then it's easy,' Opal said, lifting a squirming Guglielmo from her knee and back down on to the floor. 'You just have to convince Zane of that.'

Sure, Ruby thought, *piece of cake*, as she watched Guglielmo toddle happily over to his sister, plonk down beside her and pick up a book, too, upside-down, but not that he cared. She smiled, watching her young niece right it and hand it back before her younger brother could protest too loudly.

Both her sisters really seemed to have it all: the great careers, the drop-dead gorgeous husbands who were also their soul-mates, and, to top it off, now also beautiful families. Only this morning she'd learned the wonderful news that her sister Sapphy was expecting twin boys. By all accounts both she and husband Khaled were over the moon.

'Guglielmo's such a gorgeous baby. And he's going to look just like Domenic when he gets older, a real lady killer. And Ellie is so cute, too. Both your kids are just so beautiful.'

Opal turned her attention from the children and looked Ruby straight in the eye. 'You know, you and Zane would make beautiful babies.'

Ruby looked up sharply. *Babies?*

Then it hit her. *Zane's babies.*

How special would that be—to give him a child, a tiny Zane, maybe to build a family with him, to replace something of what he'd lost?

But it was a fantasy.

She sighed, knowing she should probably say nothing, but needing someone to confide in. 'He has mentioned marriage.'

'Oh, Ruby! That's fantastic!' Opal reached over and hugged her sister. 'Congratulations! When are you going to tell Mum?'

She shook her head. 'I told him I hadn't decided.'

Opal sat down again, stunned. 'But what on earth for? I mean, you love him, don't you?'

Ruby stared at her sister and blinked. 'Is it that obvious?'

'Come on,' her older sister said, 'Zane's not the only one putting out signals. Don't you know the way you look at him? And when you guys are together, you're both so hot it's a wonder you don't start bushfires.'

'Maybe. But that's lust and right now that's the only thing we have between us. Zane doesn't love me. He all but admitted it. He thinks we'll eventually form some kind of affectionate bond. I don't think I can do that. I can't marry a guy I love knowing he doesn't love me in return. I couldn't settle for mere affection. Look what happened to Mum, driven away, driven crazy, because she loved too much.'

Opal picked up Ruby's hand and patted it between hers, a knowing look in her eye. 'Hey, have faith! Zane loves you, I'm sure of it. But sometimes these men take a while to come to terms with being in love—maybe he just doesn't realise it yet.'

Zane tried to catch up on sleep on the flight back to Broome. There hadn't been much of that last night. He growled out a sigh and stretched back in his wide business-class seat. Just thinking about last night made him hard all over again. Ruby was honeyed perfection, inside and out. It was going to be one hell of a long week sleeping alone, waiting for her return. Maybe he should have gone with her after all, and left the pearl business to take care of itself. Maybe then she wouldn't have been so edgy.

What had that been all about?

Couldn't she understand that marriage would make so much sense? Laurence had clearly had such an outcome in mind from the start, as the perfect way to cement his young protégée to the business for ever. And what better way to get his son home and keep him there? Zane allowed himself a smile. The idea of a lifetime of nights spent with Ruby had a lot of appeal. It would never make up for what Laurence had done to his mother, but he sure had to hand it to the old man. It was one hell of a plan.

Now he just had to get Ruby to fall in with it. He closed his eyes and settled the chair to recline, crossing his arms and ankles.

She'd come around.

Could Opal be right? Ruby drove herself crazy with that question over the next few days. When she wasn't meeting with high-powered clients and agent representatives, her mind was churning, tossing around the possibilities. Only two things were certain. First, that she loved Zane, and second, that she'd happily spend the rest of her life with him if only she could be certain her love would be returned and not wasted.

But what if Opal was right and he loved her already? What were the chances? What if he didn't love her and she married him and he was never able to reciprocate that love?

Could she afford to take a risk? Should she?

In the end it was a television hostess in London who answered her question for her. Sonia Clarke was the morning television queen and already a big fan of her designs. Today she was sporting her own signature string of perfect silver-white pearls and matching earrings that she'd ordered especially from Ruby's previous collection. It was the first of a long line-up of appointments she had today before leaving later that night from Heathrow on the long flight home, an entire day earlier than expected due to a flight rescheduling. It had meant some major reorganisation of her own schedule, but she'd managed to fit everything in at a squeeze.

The interview was going well and Ruby appreciated Sonya's extensive knowledge of the industry and her appreciation for the gems. It was a good way to start the day. Then Sonia asked her why she thought her designs were so success-ful the world over. With barely a thought Ruby proceeded to go through her usual answer—she was fortunate enough to be able to work with the most beautiful pearls in the world and she'd always been given a lot of scope by Laurence to put her heart into her work. It was then that the Sonia said it.

'If you don't mind me saying so, I think your success is also due in a large way because you take such risks with your work. The Passion Collection is a case in point. Who else would imagine that a jewellery design could be so evocative, could so resemble a lovers' embrace? But you obviously achieved that because you're a risk-taker. You couldn't have done it, otherwise.'

Ruby stared blankly at Sonia and mumbled something in

response and somehow even managed to make it through the rest of the interview. But she couldn't get the words out of her head. She was a risk-taker. And it was true. She took major risks with her designs every day.

Maybe it was time to take a risk on Zane.

Ruby stepped on to the tarmac of Broome International Airport and felt the familiar heat wrap around her like a warm embrace—*a lover's embrace*. Broome had never felt so good. And she couldn't wait to surprise Zane. It was a Sunday and he'd probably be home. She wasn't even going to wait until she'd gone to her room at the hotel and freshened up. She'd go straight to the house and with any luck she could freshen up with him.

The taxi driver pulled into the driveway and helped her out with her bag. He was just pulling out on to the street when Kyoto came clambering down the stairs urgently, his aging knees angled wide over his slippered feet.

'Miss Ruby! Miss Ruby!'

It was no welcome-home greeting. 'Kyoto, what's wrong?'

Kyoto didn't have time to answer before she appeared on the verandah, all elegance and grace and Nordic swish, one hand resting gracefully on the balustrade, the other propped against an upright beam, looking to all the world like she owned the place.

'So *you're* Ruby. But aren't you home early? Zane told me we had until tomorrow.'

CHAPTER TWELVE

RUBY'S BLOOD TURNED TO ICE, frozen crystals piercing her flesh, tattooing the word '*fool*' in giant letters on her heart. The woman was beautiful, like a tall white lily, her features classical, her clothes couture, and she was so obviously not 'just an old friend' of Zane's.

And if the swell under her liquid silk gown was any indication, she was also pregnant!

Her gut churned. Oh, my God, surely it couldn't be—*Zane's baby*?

No wonder he hadn't given her a hard time over her insisting she do the overseas tour alone. He'd planned to ship his mistress in while she was gone. And after all that talk about marriage!

'You must be Anneleise,' she acknowledged. She looked searchingly over at Kyoto, his face a wrinkled mess of concern. 'Where's Zane?'

'Gone to the office,' Anneleise crooned from the verandah. 'He said he had work to do, but I'm betting he's sorting out some lovely trinkets for me. He's so thoughtful like that. He'll be back later this afternoon. Shall I tell him you dropped by?'

Ruby ignored her, trying even harder to ignore the thought of

Anneleise wearing one of her designs, having it adorn her porcelain skin, having Zane make love to her while she wore it…

'Kyoto?' she said, trying to keep balance, to maintain some kind of hold on reality. 'What's going on?'

'I'm sorry, Miss Ruby. He say she should go before you get back.'

'I'll just bet he did,' she whispered under her breath.

'It's okay, Kyoto,' crooned Anneleise, floating down the stairs like a silken viper, 'it was inevitable that we'd meet up at some stage, what with us both having Zane in common.'

If Ruby thought Anneleise looked stunning standing up on the verandah, it was nothing to how she looked close up. Fine boned and long-limbed, her almost translucent skin and silvery blonde hair gave her a fragile, almost ethereal look.

And after twenty-plus hours travelling, Ruby felt like a damp rag next to the finest silk.

Anneleise looked down at Ruby's luggage and frowned. 'Were you expecting Zane to give you a lift somewhere?'

Ruby's breath hissed through her teeth. *Not quite*, but there was no way she was staying now. Obviously she was surplus to requirements. 'Yes,' she lied. 'Just to my hotel while we talked over business. But I'll get a taxi.'

Kyoto gave her an apologetic look and bowed slightly. 'I'll call,' he said, before heading back into the house.

Anneleise placed a pale hand against her brow. 'It's so hot in the sun. I feel quite dizzy.'

Her brow pulled into a frown as Anneleise's slim-fitting dress pulled taut over her stomach as she settled herself down in the covered swing, resting one manicured hand on her tummy.

There was Zane's dynasty in waiting! All that talk about what Laurence had wanted had meant nothing. Because he didn't care what Laurence wanted—he never had. All he cared about was his blessed birthright—and he'd do anything to wrest control from her, even if he had to marry her. He'd get his shares and a convenient lay in the process. And in Sydney she'd shown him just how convenient she could be.

What a total fool she'd been!

'I really don't know how you put up with this shocking heat,' complained Anneleise, fanning her face with her hand. 'I thought it would be winter here now.'

'It is winter,' Ruby retorted, finding the day warm but by no means unpleasant. 'But here in the tropics we call it the dry.'

'Then the sooner Zane comes home to London the better. I don't think I could take too much of this. He has such a beautiful home in Chelsea. You must visit us there some time.'

Ruby sucked in a breath. It just got better and better. 'When do you think that might happen?'

'I'm not sure. Once he's sorted out some problem with the shares or something.'

Her ears pricked up. 'What problem?'

She shrugged, and even managed to do that elegantly. 'Something his father made a mess of, apparently. I don't know the details, only that it's keeping him here much longer than he intended.'

Ruby said nothing, while all she wanted to do was scream. And yell. And hit someone.

Mostly Zane.

What was the point of all that rubbish he'd spoken about them managing the business together into the future? What was all that garbage about marriage? Or was there method in his madness—to marry somebody he knew he could trust to look after the company, enabling him to flit off to Europe and his blonde bombshell whenever he felt the urge?

Or was this his way of seeking the ultimate revenge upon his father? Marry the whore and take total control without having to spend a cent.

The bitter sting of tears pricked at her eyes, but she forced them back. Damn the man! But the last thing she would let herself do was to allow herself to cry in front of his paramour.

The taxi was a welcome sight. 'It was lovely to meet you,' she heard Anneleise call from the swing as Ruby hurled both herself and her hand luggage into the car.

'Are you all packed?' Zane hoped she was. He was in no mood to put up with more of Anneleise's delaying tactics. He was in no mood to put up with Anneleise, period. He'd taken himself off to his office for hours today so he didn't have to put up with her attempts at gentle persuasion.

Anneleise pouted and reclined languidly on the swing, setting up a gentle swinging motion. 'Do I really have to go already? It's such a long journey.'

'You should have thought about that before you invited yourself here. You'll be on that plane, today.'

Before Ruby gets back! Two times now he'd thought he'd had her, he'd thought she was his for the taking, and then he'd thrown a spanner in the works and said something stupid and blown it and she'd gone cold and backed right away from him. He wasn't prepared to risk that happening again. And Anneleise made for one mighty big spanner.

'But in my condition…'

'You should have thought about that, too!'

'You were so nice to me in London.' She pouted, sounding confused. 'I thought you cared.'

'You needed help. I got you that help. I would have done the same for a sick dog.' But all the same he wished he hadn't. 'Where are your bags?'

'You had a visitor while you were out.'

'Oh,' he replied, only half-interested, thinking more about how he was going to get around the problem of admitting that

Anneleise had been here at all. Ruby had enough problems trusting him without him adding to his sins by thinking he could keep it a secret. But he'd have to pick the right time. He had too much ground to make up first. He lifted the boot of the car and looked over to the house, half-expecting Kyoto to already have her bags ready and waiting.

'So, I was thinking maybe there's no rush for me to leave after all. I mean, now that we've actually met.'

Cold dread seeped into his spine. He snapped his attention back to Anneleise, who was smiling, her eyes wide with the excitement of someone sharing a secret.

'Met who?'

'Why, your little friend Ruby, of course.'

Agony tore a swathe through him, all but wrenching his guts from his body.

'Ruby was here?'

She laughed and right at that moment he'd never heard such a sick sound or hated anyone half as much. And he'd felt sorry for her in London!

'She's quite pretty.'

He had to get to her! He slammed the boot shut.

'Kyoto!' he yelled, already halfway to the house. 'Kyoto!'

'But she seemed upset about something.'

He spun around, half-needing to know, half-dreading the answer already. 'What did you say to her?'

She eased out of the chair and glided across the lawns towards him. 'Oh, nothing in particular and nothing that you didn't tell me in London. Just how you were planning to return after you'd sorted out this business with the shares.'

My God! He could just imagine how Ruby would take comments like those. He'd still hoped to buy Ruby out back then. 'I said that *if* I returned to London it wouldn't be for some time.'

She shrugged and looked up at him innocently. 'Isn't that almost the same thing?'

Zane ignored her. He was too busy estimating the amount of damage Anneleise had done. He had no doubt her barbs were calculated, but she wouldn't have had any idea of the amount of poison they contained. She would be delighted if she only knew.

'Kyoto!' he yelled again before turning around. 'Kyoto can order you a taxi. But I want you out of here now. And I don't want to find you here when I get back.'

'But you knew I was coming. I called you when I booked!'

'And I told you to cancel!'

'So where are you going?' she demanded, her voice cracking with the inevitable tears. Not that they'd make any difference.

'Where do you think I'm going? To try and repair some of the damage you've done.'

He entered the house's cool interior, dark after the bright sunlight. Where was that man? This was no time to take a nap!

'You love her, don't you?'

Anneleise sounded angry, her attempt at tears obviously already abandoned as useless, and for a moment he was going to snap back that she was wrong, just like she was wrong thinking there was any hope of a relationship between him and her.

And then it hit him. He couldn't say that. Anneleise had for once spoken the truth. She was right.

He was in love with Ruby!

Anguish melded with fury at the revelation. How could he have not seen that until now? How could he have missed so obvious a truth?

He stormed into the kitchen, his mind in turmoil, his heart in shock, his senses blown away.

And that's when he found him.

CHAPTER THIRTEEN

CABLE BEACH SEEMED to stretch forever, disappearing into the distance in both directions, its endless white sands and brilliant turquoise sea all framed by a boundless sky. Ruby got the impression that if she just kept walking she'd disappear too, that she'd fade into the distance like the coast line. And right now the idea held a lot of appeal.

Sand whipped around her ankles and stung against her face, but it didn't matter and unlike the other beach-goers, who'd headed back to the resort when the wind picked up, she didn't try to shelter from the wind. Her eyes were already gritty and swollen, she had nothing to fear from the elements.

It was people who could wreak the most damage. People that you trusted and who let you down. It was people who inflicted the deepest cuts.

She wandered further down the deserted beach, her sandals clutched in one hand, slapping against her legs as she walked, her toes splashing in the shallows of the Indian Ocean. She didn't know how long she'd been walking. She didn't really care. And what else could she do? Sleep had eluded her. An hour of lying on her bed, seeking the bliss that only deep, dreamless sleep could provide, had shown her that.

So she walked, and she kept on walking. And only when

the sun had started to dip towards its inevitable union with the ocean did she turn around and head back to the resort.

There was no missing the flashing message button on her phone. The phone rang again and she let it ring until it rang out. If that was Zane, she didn't want to talk to him. Anybody else she didn't need to talk to right now. So she ignored it, instead stripping off and standing under a hot shower for a long time, letting the water wash away the sand-streaked tracks of her tears, wishing it could so easily wash away the bitter tracks through her heart.

Minutes later, there was a noise, a thumping. Someone was pounding on her door.

She didn't have to open the door to know who it would be. *Zane.*

Maybe if she was quiet, he'd eventually get sick of pounding. Maybe then he'd go away.

Or maybe she should just call security and have him removed. She turned off the taps and reached for a towel.

'Ruby,' she heard him yell. 'Open the door.'

She put her hands over her ears, thinking that she should turn on the taps again. It had been better when she couldn't hear his voice.

'Ruby!'

'Go away. I don't want to talk to you.'

'You have to come. It's Kyoto. He's collapsed.'

'What happened?' she asked as she buckled herself into the seat belt, studiously averting her eyes from anywhere near him. She looked a mess, her eyes puffy and red, her hair still wet from the shower, and still she was the most beautiful thing he'd seen all day. He put an arm around the back of her seat.

'Ruby, we have to talk.'

'No. Only about Kyoto!'

'But—'

She turned then and hit him with the full force of her shattered eyes. 'I thought you said we had to get to the hospital!'

The sight of her eyes, the damage he'd caused so openly displayed in their depths… His lungs felt sick and tight, but still he put the car in gear, pulling out from the car park. He'd known it wasn't going to be easy to make up for what had happened, but how the hell was he going to get her back after this?

'I found him lying in the kitchen.'

'His heart?'

'The doctors are assessing him now. It might be his heart, or it could be anything. He's old. But his condition is critical and I thought you should know.' He looked over at her. 'I was calling for hours. Where were you?'

'I went for a walk,' she said blankly.

'I'm sorry,' he said.

'I don't want to talk about it,' she replied, turning her head away.

It was too soon. Too soon to be returning to this place. Too soon to be holding another dying man's hand. She'd barely seen him over the last few weeks, too wound up about events in her own life to think about him. She should have thought about him. She should have done something! Someone placed a gentle hand on her shoulder.

'You need to leave now.'

She let herself be led from the room, feeling a blessed numbedness descend over her. Maybe that's what happened when you felt too much, she decided. Maybe she'd tripped some kind of sensory overload button and everything had shut down.

Then she took one look at Zane waiting for her in the corridor and the pain sliced right through her again.

She breathed in deep. She wouldn't let herself think about Zane. Right now she had to focus on Kyoto, on thinking positive thoughts for him. 'Will he make it?' she whispered.

Zane's expression was bleak, with not a trace of the reassurance she craved. 'They don't know, but he's very old. There may not be a lot they can do.'

Tears welled in her eyes, blurring her vision. 'Then that's Laurence gone and now maybe Kyoto, too.'

She bit down on her lips, looked down at the floor, somehow managed to squeeze out the words, 'Thank you for bringing me.'

'Come on,' he said, not touching her. 'I'll take you home.'

'No!' she said as the car pulled into the all-too-familiar driveway. 'You said you'd take me home. I want *my* home.'

'We need to talk,' he said.

'And I told you I don't want to talk. How could you even bring me here? I won't go in there, not knowing *she's* inside.'

'Anneleise is gone.'

'And that's supposed to make everything all right? The European mistress has been packed away and now it's time for the Broome mistress to take up residence again? I don't want to go inside and I don't want to talk.'

'It's not like it seems.'

'Well, I know that she's certainly not "just some old friend", like you made out.'

'I know.' He took a deep breath. 'I'm sorry. I should have told you before. We did have a brief affair. Very brief. But it was over months ago. It didn't seem important.'

'A baby isn't important?'

'You can't believe it's mine!'

'Why not? I know you spent time with her in London and then you let me take the overseas tour alone so you could sneak some time here with your mistress. Damned inconvenient for you both, with me coming back a day early. She said you'd told her you two had until tomorrow. She must have been gutted to have been shunted off tonight.'

'You think I'd do that if it was my baby? What kind of monster do you think I am?'

'A monster who'll do anything to regain a birthright he believes was stolen from him.'

He sighed, long and hard. 'Ruby, I can straighten all this out. Just give me a chance. But not here. Come inside. We both need a coffee, maybe even something stronger after the few hours. And if the hospital calls—'

'You've got a mobile.'

'That needs charging. I don't want to miss them if they call—do you?'

Inside the house she waited on one of the large living-room sofas. He handed her a coffee, their hands brushed and she shivered.

He peered more closely at her. 'Cold?'

'Yes,' she lied, not wanting him to know how much he still physically affected her, even after all he'd done to betray her trust. 'The coffee will help.'

'It's probably shock,' he offered. 'And the fact you're almost dead on your feet.'

'You were going to straighten everything out,' she said, wanting to deflect the conversation from herself. 'Maybe you ought to get started.'

He looked at her evenly. Then he sighed and sat down opposite, depositing his brandy down on the table between them.

'I met Anneleise at a dinner party. She seemed bright and intelligent and I was attracted to her. We dated a few times and, yes, we had what you'd call an affair. It was entertaining for a while, but I soon learned that there was nothing below the surface, that she was fragile emotionally and she was also very clingy. When I told her we wouldn't be seeing each other again, she refused to accept that it was over. I was hoping that being out here would finally give her the message.'

'But you saw her in London!'

'I didn't intend to. She came to me for help. She'd discovered she was pregnant by her latest lover.'

'So why didn't she go to him for help?'

'He wouldn't help her. By the time she learned I was in London she was desperate, possibly suicidal. So I found her a psychiatrist and a quiet health clinic where she could take her time and think things over. I didn't realise that by helping her I'd make her think I still cared about her. But she kept on phoning and texting. Then she arrived here yesterday. I certainly didn't want her here.'

'You make her sound like some crazy stalker!'

'Exactly.' He tilted his head. 'It seems we have something in common, wouldn't you say?'

She blinked.

'Except,' he continued, 'unlike in your case, she never threatened me physically. She was just more of a nuisance. I never felt scared of her until today, when I found out you'd come home early and you two had met.'

He held her eyes across the table.

'She's a parasite, Ruby. I'm sorry I ever met her. I'm even sorrier that you had to go through what you did. I'm sorry that I hurt you because of her. Is there any chance you can forgive me?'

His eyes were dark and troubled, and he looked more worried than she'd ever seen him, the lines of his face strained and tight. She'd seen that face, eyelids closed next to hers on the pillow, had woken with those eyes staring into hers and a kiss hovering on his lips and she so wished she could smooth those lines away now.

But it was too late.

'It doesn't matter,' she said. 'It's not just Anneleise, though, is it? It could be anyone. And this goes deeper than whether or not you have a mistress. It's what's important to you that bothers me. I just can't trust you—the things she said about you—'

He jumped to his feet. 'She lied!'

'Maybe, but what she said echoed with my own concerns about you. It's the shares you care about. You'll do anything to get hold of them.'

'That's not true!'

He was too big standing over her, too imposing. She stood up and moved away, crossing her arms protectively around her. 'You talked to her about it when you were in London! You told her you planned to return to London when you'd worked out this "problem" with the shares. This to a woman you claim is stalking you! Why would you do that?'

'It wasn't like that!'

'I was the problem with the shares, wasn't I? I have been all along. Me and my forty-five per cent. And you finally worked out what to do with me—marry me and then you could manage them all, and have whomever you wanted on the side! If not Anneleise, then whoever else was flavour of the month.'

'No! Anneleise was trying to upset you. Don't let her poison work. She said those things because she was jealous of you.'

'Why would she be jealous of me? She doesn't even know me.'

'She knew you because I talked about you in London. I spent a few hours sitting next to her bedside while she settled into the psychiatric clinic. I talked to her about Broome and about your designs and how ground-breaking they were. She obviously saw you as a threat. Not that she was ever in the running.

'But that's not the only reason she wanted to hurt you.'

'What else could there be?'

He moved closer, his dark eyes imploring, his hands palm up between them. 'Because she realised something I was too stupid to realise myself. She saw something I was blind to. And that is that I want to spend my life with you, if you'll have me. And that's why I want you to marry me.'

He reached for her hands and took them in his own and squeezed them gently.

'Because I love you.'

CHAPTER FOURTEEN

HE WATCHED THE TANGLE OF EMOTIONS rumble like wet-season storm clouds across her blue eyes. He waited, hoping that at last he'd got it right, that at last he'd done the right thing.

'Oh, no,' she said, finally wrenching her hands out of his.

He blinked. He couldn't have heard right.

'No?'

She was still shaking her head. 'No way!' She swung away. 'What is this? The latest chapter from your corporate takeover manual? "How to Marry a Major Shareholding—101".'

'What are you talking about?

'First you haven't been able to buy my shares and then you can't convince me to marry you, so now you bring out the big guns. That's what I'm talking about.'

'I love you, dammit! It happened.'

'Well, I'm sorry, Zane, but it won't work. I'm sick of the lies. I'm sick of the deception and the betrayals. I'm sick of not being able to trust you. And lying to me about loving me won't help.'

'I'm not lying. Why can't you see that?'

'What I see is that you're suddenly so anxious to marry me you'll try anything. And the only reason I can think of for marrying me is to get closer to my shareholding now that you can't buy me out and so you can control it alongside yours. To give you back the share of the company you no doubt feel you were cheated out of by your father, and because in your deluded mind you probably see it as the ultimate revenge— you were going to live your life the way you always accused your father of doing!'

'I want to marry you because I want to be with you! I want to spend my life with you. So leave my father out of this. It's got nothing to do with him.'

'Your father is the sole reason I'm here! Without him I would be long gone. Because your father was a good man, a very good man. Yes, he was hard at times, but he was a man of integrity. But you can't see that. And it affects your judgement just as it affects the type of person you are. And I have to tell you, you're not a patch on Laurence. You're not half the man he was.'

Blood crashed through his veins, thumping so loudly in his head that it was impossible to see anything but red-hot rage.

He never thought he was perfect! But to be held up next to his father like that—maybe it was time she learned more about his father than what Laurence wanted her to know.

'You think my father was perfect? You think he was beyond reproach?'

She looked at him uncertainly for a moment. Then steel resolve once again filled those blue depths. 'Laurence always acted out of integrity. I could always trust him. Always.'

'Then just take a look at this!' From the mantelpiece behind him he pulled down the chest, the box bequeathed to him, and turned the key in the tiny lock.

'What's this?' she asked suspiciously.

'Look inside,' he said. 'This is something Laurence had Kyoto hand to me especially on my return. I told you what he'd done when my mother was killed. I told you how he'd elevated his mistress to an equivalent position to my mother. And you didn't believe me.' He pulled off the lock and wrenched open the lid from the box, found the letter he wanted and thrust it toward her.

'This is what I learned when I was just a kid—that my father had set my mother's best friend up in a house of her own, conveniently just around the corner, and settled on her a monthly payment for life. And it didn't make sense until she died and I worked out why.

'Zane, I don't think—'

'Read it! You read this letter. Read them all if that's not enough—they're no doubt love letters that support what I'm saying. Read them and you tell me what you think. See how wonderful you think your mentor really was!'

So she read the letter he'd handed her, and it was just as he'd said: in return for 'services rendered', there followed the payment terms, a monthly stipend and a property.

She sat there, shocked, because Zane was right! The thing she had refused to believe—and she was staring at the proof.

'Zane,' she said, looking up to him, shaken to the core.

'Don't stop now. Read those love letters while you're there,' he said. 'Might as well know the whole sordid truth.'

Reluctantly she picked up another letter, turning it over in her hands before looking up at him. 'But it's not a love letter,' she declared once her brain had made sense of the names. 'It's from your mother to Bonnie.'

'Let me see.' Zane joined her on the couch, looked at the envelope and letter she'd handed to him, and frowned. Not love letters? But he'd thought...

He took in the Italian stamps and the faded postmark showing a date almost a year after he was born and smoothed the pages. He frowned after reading the contents, refolding the letter before picking up another, again from his mother to Bonnie, although this one was from New York, postmarked a week later. Once more he scanned the contents; once more he put it down, more confused, more irritated. After a half-dozen letters, all from different locations around the globe, Zane stopped reading.

Every letter followed the same formula, a brief introduction of where they were and her impressions and then what followed was almost a blow-by-blow description of what the young Zane was up to. 'Zane said this', 'Zane did that', 'Zane took his first steps today, I wish you'd been here to see it.'

And as he read, a prickling shiver crawled along his spine.

'They're all about you,' she whispered, 'every one of them. Reports of what you're doing, how you're growing.'

'I know,' he said, the creeping feeling of unease settling in deep between his shoulder blades.

'And did you notice how they were all signed off?'

Zane nodded, his throat suddenly ashen, the bottom in his world fast dropping away. Had she seen it, too?'

'Maree signed each one, *"from your loving friend forever"* and—' He couldn't speak, couldn't finish what he'd been going to say.

So Ruby finished it for him. 'And *"thank you so much for your precious gift"*.' She looked over at him, with pain in her eyes that must be a mere shadow compared to his own. 'I think *you* were that precious gift, Zane. And Maree was thanking Bonnie in every letter. Because Bonnie was your birth mother.'

'No!' The word exploded from him like a blast from a cannon, even though he'd been thinking the very same thing. But hearing it said, having to acknowledge it as the truth when it couldn't be…

'Bonnie was my father's mistress. She *killed* my mother.'

'Zane…' She stood, placed a hand on his arm. 'Why else would the same lines appear in every letter?'

'It's impossible.' He pulled away. 'I have a birth certificate that names Maree as my mother. There's no way Bonnie could have delivered me.'

'Maybe someone at the hospital was in on it?'

'I wasn't born here. My parents were on holiday in Italy. I arrived earlier than expected.'

Her mind ticked over with the possibilities. 'Then maybe if Bonnie was with them…'

'No maybes!' He slammed his hand down on the mantelpiece. 'It's Maree's name on my birth certificate. I don't have to believe anything else.'

She picked up more of the letters from the box and held them out to him. 'Maybe you should read more. Read them all. How many will it take before you believe?'

He blocked her hand, knocking her wrist and causing the letters to tumble, scattering over the floor.

'I don't want to read any more!' he said with his hands on the mantelpiece, his back to her. 'I can't believe it. I won't.'

Because if he did believe it, then he'd know he'd been wrong, desperately wrong about his father, about his mother, about Bonnie!

Ruby crouched down, gathering the letters up again. One on blue notepaper had separated, the pages falling to individual sheets wide apart on the floor. She picked them up, putting them together, when the different handwriting caught her eye. Familiar handwriting!

She shivered, a wave of tiny needle pricks washing over her. The letter was addressed to Zane. With a rush of exhilaration she put the pages back in order.

'Zane,' she said, holding the letter out to him, her heart

beating like a wild thing in her chest. 'I think you'll want to read this one. It's addressed to you. And it's from your father.'

He turned slowly, regarding both her and the letter with suspicion. Would it mean more madness or would his father's words show Ruby's theory to be the crackpot idea it had to be?

Her eyes urged him to take it, her attitude challenging and at the same time tender, as if she understood. *The woman I love*, he thought, knowing once again he'd blown it with her. And nothing, not anything his father might tell him from beyond the grave, could be more devastating than to know that he'd lost her.

He took the pages from her hand, then he looked down and began to read.

Dear Zane, my son,
This is a very hard letter for a father to write. But after so many years apart I know I must write this down, so you might read it together with the letters from Maree to Bonnie and understand once I am gone. And, one day, you might even forgive me.

The truth is, I should have told you many, many years ago. But I waited too long. Liked the way things were. It was easier. Everyone was happy. We knew that one day you would have to find out the truth, but we put that day off.

But then both Maree and Bonnie were killed together and suddenly the time to let you know was past.

Iron manacles clamped down on his gut, squeezing him tight inside, squeezing the air from his lungs. He collapsed down on to the sofa and continued to read.

You see, while your mother, Maree, raised you and

brought you up as her own child, it was Bonnie who gave birth to you. Maree so desperately wanted children and I wanted a son, just one son. Maree endured five miscarriages, the last one causing complications that meant she could never have children. She was devastated. And I was powerless to help her.

It was Bonnie who came up with the plan. Bonnie saw what it was doing to Maree. She saw that it was destroying her. She wanted to do something to help her friend and the only way she could was to offer her a child that she herself had borne.

I was against it. I didn't want anything to come between Maree and me. I loved her so much. I know you doubted that, but she meant more to me than anything.

But Maree embraced the idea. She wanted it to work and believed it would work—even their looks were similar, both with dark hair and eyes—who would ever know? And so the women calculated the best time and I slept with Bonnie. In all my years, it was the hardest thing I have ever done. Until they both died it is the only time I ever cried. But thank God, it worked. She fell pregnant with that first attempt. I was relieved. Maree was overjoyed. It was a miracle, she said, with hope in her eyes for the first time in years.

Zane's eyes lifted from the page. 'You were right,' he said, his voice flat, belying the paradigm shift going on in his mind and soul. 'Bonnie was my mother. My father slept with her but only once. She wasn't his mistress at all. And all those years…'

All those years he'd damned his father. And he'd damned Bonnie, wonderful, warm Bonnie with her wide smile, always ready to give him a hug or soothe him when he fell over or to encourage him at school—he'd loved her all the years of growing up and then he'd damned her all the rest as being Laurence's mistress. He'd never had the chance to tell her how much she meant to him. He hadn't even hung around long enough to see her buried!

And she was his mother!

Anguish tore at him, leaving the tattered shreds of his soul hanging out to dry.

He hadn't known. He'd never suspected. And now it was too late!

He dropped his head into one hand as he read on.

The women went to live in the village I came from for the few weeks before you were born. The local midwife, a cousin of mine, delivered you. It was no hardship to register Maree as the mother.

Any hesitation I had had about the whole plan ended that day. Maree finally had achieved her dream, a baby in her arms. And I had my son!

I bought Bonnie a house close by to ours. She didn't want it, she didn't want any payment, she'd done this for Maree out of love for her, but Maree and I insisted. So you grew up, surrounded by the love of both Bonnie and Maree, both of them loving you, the women now closer than ever. And one day, I told myself, one day I will tell Zane the truth and he will know. But Maree loved so much being your mother that I couldn't do it to her. Not until she was ready for it. She was so proud to call herself your mother, so proud to have you for her son.

And you loved Bonnie so much, anyway, I thought it didn't really matter, that you couldn't love her any more if she were your mother. Except it did matter. And when they died together that day, I knew I'd waited so long that there was no point telling you at all. You would only hate me for not telling you, hate me for the deception, hate me for the chance of not knowing Bonnie as your birth mother and being able to acknowledge that fact.

And you did hate me. I was angry at the time, very angry as you no doubt remember, but in the end it doesn't matter that you were angry at me for the wrong reasons. I deserved your anger. You took yourself away from Broome and I accepted your scorn as my punishment. In a way I think I lost you when I lost both the love of my life and the mother of my child. But I was always, always, so very proud of you.

He read the rest through a film of moisture blurring the words but not the emotion, eventually sighing, putting the letter down, leaning back in his chair, one hand rubbing his brow.

'Zane?'

He opened his eyes and she was there, leaning over him all beautiful and intent like an angel. 'I made you a warm drink. I thought you might need it.'

He hadn't even realised she'd left the room and now she was back, taking care of his needs. He almost told her he loved her again, the words almost leaving his lips. But he couldn't do it. He couldn't risk making her angry again. He had no wish to upset her, not when he already had so much to apologise for; and, after tonight's revelations, well, now there was so much more.

'Thank you,' he said, taking a sip of the brandy-laced coffee. It was good, warming him momentarily in places so recently left cold and bereft.

And then he thought of something else he could say. Something that he'd never believed, but tonight had learned was true, and something that she couldn't object to hearing. 'My father was a good man,' he said. 'I wish I'd realised that earlier.'

'Oh, Zane,' she said, tears springing up in her eyes. 'Yes, he was.'

'I want to read the rest of these letters. Can you wait for me to take you home? And I want you to read Laurence's letter, seeing that you're the one who worked it all out. Maybe you can find anything else I've missed.'

She smiled and curled herself into the sofa opposite. 'Only if you're sure. And, yes, I can wait.' He handed the blue sheets over to her.

'I won't be long,' he told her, pulling the pearler master's box closer to him and gathering the next batch.

Letter after letter followed a similar formula Ruby and he'd both seen used before. Only, now he read them not as a report of what he was doing, but as a relaying of his child-hood holidays through the eyes of the woman who was his legal mother to the woman who gave birth to him. And, from reading them, it was obvious Maree and Bonnie shared an incredible bond.

He thought he'd reached the end, the last envelope, but there was something at the bottom of the chest he almost missed until he was placing everything back in again. A postcard. He pulled it out. Looked at the picture, complete with tattered corners and creased edges. Disneyland Los Angeles. He remembered that holiday. He'd been eight years old. What had Maree written about that?

Then he turned it over and with a shock recognised his own early scrawl.

Dear Aunty Bonnie,
Disneyland is great, but I miss you heaps.
I love you lots and lots,
from Zane.

Thank God! Whatever had happened after she'd died, he'd loved Bonnie when he was growing up and he *had* told her. Here was evidence that she knew just how much. At least as an eight-year-old he'd known how to express his feelings successfully.

So just when had he lost that talent?

He put the postcard down and noticed Ruby lying down, her head on a cushion, her face tranquil at last and her hair in wavy abandon around her face. She'd given up on waiting for him and fallen asleep, but that was no surprise after travelling halfway around the world, only to come home to what must have seemed like hell today. His heart both swelled and stung at the same time at the sight of her. He loved her, but she didn't want him. Why couldn't he communicate so succinctly to her as he could in a postcard when he was only a child? Why was it so hard now to say what was in his heart?

He didn't want to disturb her by removing her to a bed. The sofa was wide and comfortable, so he grabbed a light blanket and tucked it lightly over her, taking heart when he lightly kissed her cheek to see her sweet lips dance slightly to the movement even in her sleep.

'Goodnight, Ruby.'

The phone woke her, startling her all the more because she couldn't remember going to bed, because she didn't immediately know where she was.

She sat up on the sofa, pulling with her the blanket Zane must have tucked around her as she padded to the kitchen. He was already there, holding the receiver and listening intently.

Kyoto! It had to be news. She swayed against the granite bench, grateful for its support.

He put the phone down and looked at her. 'That was the hospital,' he said, confirming her fears.

She moved a step closer, her fingers anchoring her to the bench, afraid to let go. 'And?'

He took a breath, his lips curving into a smile of relief. 'His condition has improved. He's off the critical list. They're still not sure what happened, they need to run more tests, but at this stage they're hopeful he'll pull through.'

Thank God! Ruby threw herself against him in relief, wrapping her arms around him. 'Oh, Zane! That's wonderful news.'

His hands circled her, gently squeezing, gently stroking, his head dipping to hers. She felt him kiss her hair, then rest his head on hers, breathing deeply.

He smelt so good, freshly showered. He *felt* so good, and that familiar tension began to build between them, the awareness that a consolatory hug was turning into something else, something more. She drew in a breath, uncertain, unsure of where they were headed, but knowing that this journey was not over yet. Not until the air was cleared between them.

'I'm sorry,' she said, her face buried in his chest, where it was easier to admit she'd been wrong.

His hands stilled at her back. 'What have you got to be sorry for?'

'For comparing you to your father. For not believing he might be capable of deceiving you.'

'I was so wrong, though. It wasn't anything like I thought.'

'But he let you believe it, and that shaped how you acted and how you felt. Believing what you did drove your actions. What he'd done gave you no choice. And I refused to see that. I didn't trust you.'

'And...now?'

She breathed in deep, savouring his scent, letting it feed into her. 'I should have trusted you. I can't believe Laurence let you believe what you did.'

'I can,' he said. 'He'd known that one day I should be told, but he waited too long—he didn't want anything to come between my mother and me. And when they both died together, there was no point telling me. It was too late for me to acknowledge Bonnie as my birth mother and I'd probably only hate him for the deception.'

'But you hated him anyway.'

'I know. I suspect he never forgave himself for sleeping with Bonnie. My leaving was his punishment.'

'Oh, Zane, I'm so sorry.'

'I'm the one who should be sorry,' he said. 'I put you through hell, believing you and my father—'

'Hush,' she whispered. 'I let you believe it. I could have corrected you at any time, but I didn't.'

He pushed her away enough to look into her face. 'But why would you want me to believe that?'

'Because I was scared of you.' She saw the change in his features and shook her head firmly. 'No. Not like my stalker—never like him. You scared me in a different way— because there was something about you from the very beginning that was like a magnet to me. I was drawn to you and I couldn't understand why. I wanted to hate you and yet I couldn't ignore that every time you touched me I craved more. So I let you believe what you wanted to believe. It suited me to have you believe I was off-limits. It protected me. Until the launch, when I thought I'd be leaving and I just wanted one chance—one night with you before I left.'

'Thank you,' he said, through a smile tinged with sadness. 'It doesn't in any way mitigate the wrong I did you, but thank you.'

Then he pulled her close into him and squeezed her tight, lifting her from the floor, his mouth in her hair, his breath warm and welcoming.

'We have unfinished business,' he growled, putting her down again. 'But right now we have something else to take care of.'

'Can we visit Kyoto?' she asked.

'That's where we're going first. Then there's something else I have to do.'

No onshore breezes permeated this far inland today. The air felt scorching, just to breathe it in seemed to burn the lungs and crack the lips, but Zane barely noticed the conditions. He had far more important things on his mind.

In his arms were the flowers he'd picked up in town to supplement the bright cuttings of bougainvillea he'd brought from home. He hadn't been back here since his father's funeral and then he'd never looked in this direction. He'd never seen the stone, he'd never read the words. But today he did.

Today he knelt down at the side of the grave of the woman that had given birth to him. He touched the sun-warmed stone, ran his hands over its smooth surface, the thick roughened edges; he traced the words of her name etched into the marble and the date of her death and he told her he was sorry.

He placed flowers on her grave and then he did the same on the grave alongside, the grave where the woman he'd grown up believing to be his mother lay, saying a few words to her, too.

Ruby watched him from the shade of a tree as he moved to the third, as yet unfinished, grave that she knew to be his father's. She hadn't realised he'd been intending to come here after visiting Kyoto, who was barely conscious but so happy to see them, but typically so apologetic for causing so much trouble.

She'd helped Zane cut the bougainvillea, assuming they were to take to the hospital. She watched with tears in her eyes as he hunkered down and said something she couldn't hear. Then she saw him push something in the ground, something small, before smoothing the surface over again.

Then he stood and turned towards her, and her world stilled. She could see the sheen on his eyes, she could feel his pain and suddenly she knew what Laurence had meant when he'd made that final request.

Look after Zane.

He'd known what learning the truth would do to him. He'd known what the impact would be. And he'd wanted her, *wanted Ruby*, there to pick up the pieces.

He came up to her, his eyes sending signals she couldn't ignore, she couldn't help but reciprocate, the heat she was feeling now less to do with the temperature. She opened her mouth to say something, but he stopped her.

'No,' he said, his voice like a silken thread, tugging at her senses. 'Let's not talk. Not yet.'

He drove them back to the house and this time she didn't protest, didn't make a sound, because she understood what they were doing there.

Without a word, their eyes and bodies doing all the communicating, he took her hand and led her to his room. Then and only then he took her face in his hands, his fingers stroking her neck, and he kissed her. Deeply. Movingly. A kiss that said a thousand words and more. A kiss that moved her world.

Then slowly, languorously, they undressed each other, with the pace of those that know they have for ever. Each garment discarded bringing new discoveries. Each uncovering of flesh a revelation, like it was the first time.

And in a way, it was.

She soothed him, her hands conforming to every dip, every line of his body. She comforted him. The touch of her hands, the heated embrace of her mouth, even the slide of her body against his, all of these were her instruments of healing. Making up for the hurt. Banishing the bitter past.

She took care of him.

And his kisses were so tender, his touch so sweet that it almost brought tears to her eyes. And when he entered her it did. Tears of happiness. Tears of love. Tears that dissolved into stars as he took them both over the brink.

'I love you,' she whispered, as they lay still locked together in the heated aftermath. His ragged breathing stilled, his head lifted.

'What did you say?'

She looked into his face and smiled up at him, smiled at the confusion she'd wreaked there. 'I said, I love you.'

'You do?'

She smiled and nodded back. 'Oh, yes. With all my heart.'

He blinked. 'When did this happen?'

'I realised it the morning after we made love in Sydney. The new day told me I loved you.'

'Why didn't you tell me?'

'I couldn't, not after what you'd said about not needing love. I thought there was no hope for us then.'

'And I didn't tell you until last night, when I'd finally accepted the truth myself.'

She sighed. Was that only last night? It seemed like so much had happened in such a few short hours. 'Sometimes I felt that you felt something for me, but at other times...'

'You didn't trust me.'

'I'm sorry,' she said.

He took her hand in his and kissed her fingertips. 'I didn't merit your trust. Not then. I knew that I wanted you, but I didn't know why. I was caught between you and too many demons from the past.'

'And now?'

'Those demons have well and truly been laid to rest. I've made my peace with my father. I've made my peace with my mother—both of them. And now, now there's only you.' He pressed both her hands together between his own. 'I was desperate yesterday when I thought I'd lost you for ever. Nothing compared to that sense of loss. Nothing could ever be that devastating again.'

'I was upset,' she said. 'I was coming back to tell you I'd decided to give your crazy marriage plan a shot. I was determined I'd make you fall in love with me eventually.'

He dropped his head. 'I'm so sorry. I can't imagine how bad you must have felt walking back and finding—'

'Shh,' she said, hushing him. 'I don't want to talk about that. There's something I don't understand.'

'What is it?'

'At the cemetery, I saw you place something in your father's grave. What was it?'

He made a low rumbling sound as he exhaled. 'It was the lock and key from the pearl chest.'

'The one that held the letters? But…why?'

'It probably seems mad, but I needed to do it. Because the time for locking away the past is over. That only leads to bitterness and deceit. I can't change what's happened, but from now on there'll be no more secrets. Only the truth.'

'Then tell me the truth,' she invited, applauding his words and his actions. 'I want to hear you say it again. This time I intend to believe it.'

His eyes narrowed, glinted.

'I love you, Ruby. With all my heart and all my soul. I love you for ever.'

She breathed in, her heart swelling large and proud. 'And

I do believe you. Because I love you, too. And, yes, I will marry you.'

His head tilted in question.

She pouted playfully. 'You *do* still want to marry me, don't you?'

'Of course I do, but I didn't want to rush you.'

'But I want to rush. I don't want our babies to be born out of wedlock.'

'Babies?' he asked, as she pulled his head closer for a kiss.

'Oh, yes, lots and lots of babies. You're going to sire a great dynasty of Bastianis.'

His face paused just above her own. 'I like the sound of that.'

She smiled under his lips. 'In that case we better get started right away.'

'Oh,' he growled, rolling her underneath him, 'I couldn't agree more.'

EPILOGUE

CHRISTMAS WAS A NOISY AFFAIR, the whole family gathered in one of Clemengers Boutique Hotel's elegant sitting rooms after the ceremony in the Chapel that had seen Ruby and Zane's hasty marriage blessed and that had felt like a second wedding ceremony to them both.

Sapphy had designed Ruby's gown for the occasion, a gloriously rich silver-blue design that accented Ruby's eyes and that had her looking spectacular as she walked down the same aisle her sister Opal had more than five years previously.

It had been so long since all three sisters had been together and now they weren't just three sisters any more. Opal was there with Domenic and their two children, Ellie and Guglielmo; Sapphy and Khaled, who had come over in their private jet from Jebbai together with their brand new twin boys, Amid and Kahlil; and the three sisters' mother, Pearl, was there, lapping up the experience of being a grandmother four times over.

If Kyoto had been up to travelling they would have brought him to Sydney, too, but he was happy to be home, frail but thankfully alive and still insisting on running the household.

Gifts were exchanged, Christmas gifts and belated wedding presents. Ruby had also made special gifts for them all. To Opal she gifted a necklace of golden pearls and dazzling opals; a stunning pair of sapphire-and-pearl earrings went to twin Sapphy, and to her mother she gave a lush necklace, featuring baroque pearls interspersed with the three gemstones for which she'd named her daughters, opal, ruby and sapphire. Cufflinks would grace the mens' shirtsleeves.

Ellie proudly showed her bracelet of small keshi pearls to anyone and everyone and little Guglielmo just ate sandwiches, played with his new toys and wondered what all the fuss was about.

Zane reached for his new wife when she'd finished handing out the gifts, pulling her sideways on to his lap proprietarily and hauling her in close, welcoming the feel of her lush body under his hands, suddenly wishing they were somewhere more private so he could feel more. Just lately it seemed she'd looked more beautiful than ever. 'Well done,' he said, his lips pressed close against her throat. 'Once again your designs prove you're a star. You're not only beautiful, my talented wife, you're brilliant.'

She snuggled against him. 'Then I hope you don't change your mind when you open this one. I made it myself.'

Her eyes twinkled with mischief up at him, the small package held in her hand, a golden ribbon securing it.

He cursed his stupidity. They'd exchanged presents before they'd left Broome: for her a gleaming silver Mercedes, for him a forty-foot yacht called the *Bonnie Maree*, a total surprise and one that had once more brought tears to his eyes. He'd had no idea she was planning on something extra. 'But I don't have anything for you.'

'Yes, you do,' she whispered knowingly. 'You've already given it to me.' She lifted one of his hands from where it rested over her thigh, placing it low over her abdomen. 'In here is your gift. The most precious gift of all. Your gift of love.'

Blood pumped in his veins, singing wildly as it danced a

proud celebratory beat through him. 'A baby,' he said, the awe he was feeling infusing his voice.

'Your baby.'

'*Our* baby,' he growled, pulling her down till she was sitting low in his arms, close to him. 'I love you,' he told her. 'I love you so much.'

'I know,' she replied, trusting his words implicitly because she knew them to be true. 'I love you, too.'

And then he kissed her, a kiss that said I love you and thank you and for ever, over and over again.

Sapphy noticed first. 'Hey, you two, is something going on over there?'

Ruby laughed as reluctantly they broke off the kiss.

'Well?' said Zane, looking questioningly at her. 'Shall we tell them?'

Ruby smiled back at the man she loved. 'No secrets,' she said. 'Not now, not ever.'

He looked at her in respect and wonder and loved her all the more. And then he kissed her once again, just to make sure she knew it, before together they told them their news.

REQUEST YOUR FREE BOOKS!

2 FREE NOVELS PLUS 2 FREE GIFTS!

HARLEQUIN®

Blaze®

Red-hot reads!